The
SOUNDS OF
SILENCE ARE
THE LOUDEST

Cortina Jackson

The Sounds of Silence Are the Loudest

Copyright © 2018 by Cortina Jackson

ISBN: 978-0-9908862-2-8

Cover Design: Kevin Vain from CoLAB Creative Group, LLC

Edited by Aaron Baldwin

I would like to dedicate this book to my parents, Bufus and Joyce Lee. Thank you for preparing me for life's lessons, and praying for me when the lessons of life challenged my preparation. I love you so much.

To my sons Shay and Quay,

I took the wisdom and knowledge that was imparted in me, and passed it on to you. You guys took it, and soared. So proud of you!

Thank you, to all of my family and friends who supported me, and believed in my dreams, even when I was unsure. I could not have done this without you.

The evocative night air seemed to summon spirits that would later fill the streets with every ghastly deed imaginable. This was, of course, the objective the demons that inhabited the boiling inferno of Hell sought to achieve. The non-stop activity, and torment in Hell brewed over, as the evil could not be contained, in its already tight confines. The daily influx of souls entering Hell caused it to widen and deepen.

However, the influx of doomed souls was never enough for the ruler of the underworld. Greed for the annihilation of civilization was sought with a vengeance. Satan hated good, he hated fairness, and held total disdain for hope. Thus he worked day and night to make sure demons were dispatched to Earth to continue the cycle of hopelessness, sin, destruction, and death; until all experienced the molten and rotting cesspool of Hell, of which there was no return.

Wrathful demons began to emerge from portals that led from Hell to the Earth; their rotting flesh emitted a malodorous stench that sickened the strongest stomach. Their faces were hideous and terrifying to look upon; causing gut-wrenching fear that consumed the soul, rendering a person unable to stand; for the fear alone was torturous and their deeds were unfathomable.

The demons knew their assignment, they would not falter. Otherwise, their fate held the most gruesome torture imaginable. Agony took place continuously. Screaming and begging gained momentum, until it swirled into a fiery roar of its own, making it just as painful to hear, as the incinerator of fire that was felt; rushing through like a mighty wind, burning and blistering souls in its unavoidable path. Walking through just a section of Hell would make any unfortunate visitor experience cataleptic fear, inexplicable pain, and sadness. For any measure of peace, love, and joy was melted away in the boiling, liquefied sea of forgetfulness; as no one would ever remember happier times.

There are numerous divisions of Hell, but within those divisions were many sections, where the most abhorrent activities took place. Many have heard the saying, "there is a special place in Hell for you," and it became a tragic, realized statement; people who entered its confines experienced the most painful and terrifying torture, according to their sins on Earth, with each section more horrifying than the next.

There is a particular section in Hell set aside for demons who failed their assignments. This section invokes fear within the feared. Large devils are commanders here, and orchestrate punishment upon the vilest demons. Devils ravenously rip and tear the flesh off of the insubordinate demons, consuming their flesh, thus making the devils stronger and more powerful. With their extended fingertips that narrowed to a razor sharp point, they would pick, the now exposed veins, tendons, ligaments, intestines, and anything else that could be pulled out and separated. The devils gleefully play with the demon's stringy innards, like an unwound ball of yarn intertwined between playful fingers. The demons are dangled off of the ground, held up by fibrous guts that had not yet been sliced through.

However, the tissues would eventually give way, leaving the demon to fall to the ground, with ghouls feasting upon the bloody mess that spilled out. Once there was nothing left but a bloody mound, the devils allow voracious dogs to lap up whatever remained, only leaving the head. This did not mean the end of the demon, for they never have the luxury of meeting their death. The dogs and ghouls regurgitate the hot, putrid mass, and the commander devil restores life to the demon. They re-live this moment of torture repeatedly. The only break is the rush of burning flames bellowing throughout Hell, roasting everything in its path. The heat causes the skin to bubble, charring it to a crisp; only enough for the torture to begin again.

The pain is grueling; for the demons experience the pain in the same manner as a human. Every nerve, pain receptor, and synapse, is intact, and magnified 100 times, so they understood how failure and defeat really feel. The eyeballs of the demon are pierced, gouged out, and squeezed between the fingers of the devil that looks on, as the torturous merriment takes place. This would be a worthy punishment for failing an assignment.

Every now and then, Satan himself would allow a demon a chance at redemption, and it was allowed to go back out on assignment. However, the demon was admonished not to fail again, or the torture would be worse. No one, or nothing escaped Hell by death; it was a cyclical rebirth of soul trembling persecution, causing all to beg for death. Therefore, when Satan spoke,

"Do on Earth as it is in Hell," demons, imps, evil spirits, and the like, complied without hesitation.

They clawed their way from the depths of Hell, showing no mercy when entering the body and mind of all creatures upon the Earth. When an afflicted person called upon the name of Jesus for help, the evil entities experienced a piercing pain through their eardrums, like a scalding dagger sliding easily through gelatin.

The excruciating pain drove them away trembling in fear and pain; yet, they would wait for just a little break in faith, so that they could return, never giving up. The consideration of facing an angry Master was a sufficient impetus.

However, if a person continued to call Jesus, and eagerly sought Him in their trouble and despair, the evil spirit had to leave; for no evil can stand against the power of God. Everything bows and honors Him, even diabolical evil. For God is all powerful, and Satan and his henchman know that they cannot win against Him.

Even with the sheer terror of failing an assignment and returning to the anger of Satan; demons feared Christ most of all. As much as they wanted to win the battle, they could not stand against the power of God.

So, the demons operated through anything and anyone who would turn against God. People on Earth were the perfect vessels, because they experience failures in life that make them question anything good. What was good anymore? It seemed that the good guy finishes last, evil always wins, and failure is prevalent. With the minds of people so consumed, disappointed, and distraught; evil spirits would find willing participants, who go against what is right, what is just, what is righteous, and what is godly; thus making the evil spirit's assignments easily fulfilled.

There arose from the very pits of Hell, the demon known as Maniac. This demon brought about death through homicide, genocide, murder; and any heinous act resulting in death against another. Maniac was the ruler of legions, for his reign resulted in many frenzied subordinates willing to do his handiwork. Their merriment was disturbing; the more creative and heinous the death, the more the maniacal beings delighted in their work, prideful at what they created.

They laughed hysterically, clapped their hands, and stomped around with the most menacing grins, that seemed to be painted wide on their faces; a wretched sight to behold. The roles in Hell were delegated, and the assignments were clearly distinguished. Portals continued to open and close like a sphincter, squeezing out demons that clamored their way to the openings, waiting to be pushed through to the Earth. They spilled out onto the Earth's surface, eagerly looking for souls to enter, waiting for vulnerabilities, searching for breaks in faith, and creating strongholds to keep their position on Earth secured. Their destination was far-reaching; the effects of their atrocities spewed out, and ruined lives.

The minions assigned under Maniac took their role very seriously, for if they planned their debauchery just right, they could take countless amounts of lives, while they were yet in their sins; which would result in an immediate assignment to Hell. These demons planned their attacks carefully, hoping that the strategy paid huge dividends of death and destruction; a victory in Hell.

A feat of this magnitude pleased Maniac, and kept the assigned demons moving throughout the Earth. They sought people of all kinds, and in many different states of mind; anyone could be used as vessels. There are many people who could be easily influenced. Some due to unfortunate circumstances in their lives, others who had everything to live for, but wanted more of what life had to offer.

There were greedy, power hungry, poor, rich, lazy, curious, Christians, and non-Christians. It did not matter. If their heart and mind could be penetrated and controlled, the demons tried their best to make an impact that meant costly consequences in the lives of the host.

The demons used the body like a puppet, and when the person was no longer useful, they quickly destroyed and discarded the person, leaving tragedy, dismay, or death in its place. Just as quickly as the demons came, they left, moving on to the next evil deed, so their reign on Earth would be long. They set the ground work for other demons to fulfill their assignments. This second wave of demons swooped in for the carnage left behind by the advancing guard; carnage that took the form of depression, distrust, anger, fear, hate, and all other forms of defeat in people's lives.

All leading up to the big day when Satan would come, and rule the world. For there was an evil plan to destroy everything and everyone; the day when Satan would reveal himself to the Earth for all to see. If everything went as planned, and there was not enough praying people left on the Earth, there would be nothing anyone could do to stop him; and the people claimed by the evil forces, would be under Satan's hoofed feet in Hell, where he would rule over them for eternity.

A team of ghastly demons gathered just before their ascension into the earthly realm. One of them spoke,

"I have my eyes on a special person. He will be born of meager conditions. We will stay with him, and mold him to be our soldier, for his influence will affect many."

Just then Maniac stepped in, overhearing the plan.

"If you fail," he spoke, "I will torture you myself."

His snakelike eyes narrowed, as his forked tongue darted in and out of his swollen lips. He tasted the air, as his appetite for evil made him ravenous for more malevolence. He let out a shrill scream that reminded those under his rule, that they could not come back empty-handed. They all fell to their knees, weak with fear.

"Do not fail," he reminded them once more, angry at the very thought of Jesus and his angels winning this battle.

Just like all things living in existence, the horrific events set to occur had to be birthed. A process that came from conception, to birth, to growth, until it was manifested; complete with all of life's lessons. This evil was to be vomited onto the Earth, so that its stench and infectious sickness would spread to people who were susceptible to its vileness. This evil decay would be the very demons under the tutelage of Maniac. They were confident, evil, and unflinching, as they set their sights on a master plan sure to bring the Earth to its knees; it was destined to lead to annihilation, aided by a nation that hopefully forgot God. The conception began, in hopes that something more sinister would be birthed in the future.

"We will not fail Master," the demons promised, as they began to plan out their depravity; and in an instant, legions were formed, and they quickly spilled out onto the Earth to begin their reign.

Unsuspecting people's souls were penetrated, and they began to partake in deeds considered, demonic; for human against human depravity was unfathomable, and attempts to find peace in a corrupt world was futile. Evil abounded, and fear kept the masses from speaking out; and the sounds of silence were the loudest.

Chapter 1

She tip-toed carefully, so as not to make a sound; inevitably, the crunch of broken glass underneath the sole of her worn out Keds broke the deafening silence. She paused, her foot slightly raised, so as not to create any more shards that would reveal her presence. It was very dark, rainy, and dirty in the alleyway; that provided feigned shelter from the passing cars that seemed to stalk her, like the thickly hovering fog that eventually encompassed the night air.

As the chilling rain hit the hot pavement, steam rose in a cloud of ominous wisps that playfully danced, and then dissipated into the night sky. She chose her next steps carefully, as she spotted a dumpster just a few yards away. She took a deep breath, wiped the water that streamed down her face, and into her eyes and proceeded slowly, so as not to be spotted. She knelt beside the receptacle, and although the stench of rotting food, and trash wafted from it, it was the most peaceful and welcome place at that moment.

She sat there rocking back and forth, as she embraced her knees, pulling them into her tiny chest. She did whatever she could to keep warm; however, the violent shivering was reminding her that this was impossible. It was now that she could assess her damages.

The water from the sky now mixed with the blood on her knees as it trickled down and pooled into the creases of her arms. Scratches to her hands, defensive wounds to her arms, and a deep laceration to the side of her head now became realized, allowing her to experience tremendous pain. Her body began to tremble more, but it was not from the cold, it was from fear.

The streets were no place for a 14-year-old girl at this time of night. However, in her eyes 14 was the new 21; and she had the street smarts to get her through any situation, or so she thought.

"I don't want to die," she whispered, wondering exactly where she was.

She began to feel cold all over, and extremely weak; before she knew it, she had passed out.

***

He was a man, same as any man; he put his pants on one leg at a time, just like anybody else. He had his ritual though, that he stuck to every morning. He got up, made a pot of coffee; swallowed down about 5 cups as he surfed the internet, and then off to work. He'd throw a stick of gum in his mouth, which he would trade for a new piece every 30 minutes. It kept his nerves intact. He whistled throughout the day, and mostly kept to himself. Co-workers described him as quiet, a loner; maybe a little quirky at times, but he got the job done, and he was very good at it. When he was off work, he demanded that his time be respected. Therefore, no one bothered him; and this suited him well, as he trolled the streets partaking in his favorite merriment, serial killing.

He was very good at it too. He knew the right things to say, the right way to behave; he was very smart, charming, and good looking. Not the hunchback, with the eye in the middle of his forehead, and horns, like people expect a serial killer to appear. His whistled rendition of, "Silent Night," could have earned him a Grammy, but he was motivated instead to be an all-star in the sport of the kill.

He had a winning streak; he had never been caught, and no one ever got away, until tonight! He thought this one would be another dumb one; and she was. He would pose as an ambitious impresario with connections to some hot celebrity; with promises to get a young girl in a concert for free, or a young boy some type of record deal, or money-making opportunity. Additionally, he would promise love, protection, food, jewelry; whatever it took to gain their trust and compliance.

It was so easy to figure out what the bait would be for catching the attention of unsuspecting juveniles. Apparently, their problems were big enough to warrant the love and company of a complete stranger, who could walk the walk, and talk the talk.

This was certainly his young victim's story. She hated her parents; although they gave her everything that she wanted or needed. Who knew, why she hated them.

"Who cares?" he thought. She took the bait, that's all that mattered.

She always told social media her problems, just like the others. The internet made finding victims to kill so easy. It almost took the fun out of a good old fashion hunt. Although, the girl tonight brought back the thrill of the chase, because she managed to get away. He wasn't angry that she hit him in the mouth, distorting his ability to whistle his favorite song without some distress; he was angry at his sloppiness, he was always so careful.

It didn't matter if she got away; he had all the information that he needed to know about her. She posted pictures everywhere on all the social media sites; the pictures revealed her exact locations. She gave updates about where she was going, and who she was going with; she constantly updated everyone as to what she was doing almost every minute of the day. He knew where she lived, where she went to school, her favorite hangout, her parents' names; everything.

He was patient; when he was ready to kill her, he would kill her. She got away this time, but she was a teenager; an update to her status was inevitable, and he would be the first to know, along with the rest of the world.

He un-wrapped a stick of gum, shoved it into his mouth, and began chewing hard and fast; only the gum kept his teeth from cracking from the pressure of his clenching jaws. He began to laugh; a little chuckle at first, and then a hysterical, yet maniacal guffaw. As the laugh simmered down, a sinister grin emerged, and he began to whistle the tune, "Silent Night," as the blood sprayed from his lips onto the steering wheel. The tune always kept him from all-out insanity. He then drove home to return to his same ritual.

***

"She's waking up," the girl heard someone say, through the ringing in her ears.

"Where am I?" she said, very confused, but relieved.

She realized that she was safe now, as the team of smiling nurses and doctors gave her comfort and confirmation.

"You are going to be ok, honey. You escaped a horrific ordeal, but it's going to be ok."

"Did they get him, did they get the man that tried to kill me?" she asked.

"If you are up to it, we will let you speak with one of the detectives," the doctor spoke, not wanting to reveal more than his scope of professionalism would allow.

She agreed, and a detective walked in and sat down, as the hospital staff excused themselves.

"Ma'am, we think that you were the potential victim of a serial killer that we have been tracking for some time," the detective said. "Hopefully, you can shed light on the situation. I have my very best detective on this. He has solved many cases, and I'm confident that he will catch the monster that did this to you."

Detective Bigsby walked into the room.

"Here he is now! We call him Biggs, because he has the biggest heart in the whole department," the first detective said with a smile.

"Hello sweetheart, I'm Bigsby," the detective introduced himself. "I will be working your case; so relax, take your time, and tell me everything that you can remember."

Bigsby pulled out a recorder, his pen, and a pad, and began setting up for the interview.

"Biggs," the first detective announced, "I'll get us some coffee, be right back."

The girl was quiet, as the detective looked around, and assessed the room. He then removed his jacket and hat, giving them a shake, to knock off some of the rain. He took his seat next to the hospital bed, as he reached into his pocket, and pulled out a stick of gum, that replaced the piece before it. The girl looked at him in horror, as he smiled, and began to whistle the best rendition of, "Silent Night" she had ever heard, good enough to earn him a Grammy.

Chapter 2

As dawn turned into dusk, a city that would not sleep was peered upon by the eyes of God, who watched vicious attacks unfold before His eyes, yet another night. That night, a dark figure would appear in a neighborhood, prowling meticulously, as he stared into the open and inviting windows of unsuspicious occupants. They never realized that they were only a hairsbreadth away from being the next victim of a brutal killer's hideous intentions.

Most people never realized they stared serial killers right in the eyes daily. The walked by them, answered questions for directions, or the time; gave them rides in their vehicles, never understanding the magnitude of what could befall them.

Tonight was no exception, as curtains were wide open in this neighborhood. A neighborhood where the false sense of security, initiated from the belief that locked doors provided safety from outside dangers, comforted the occupants. The car hardly made a sound, as it slowly crept by trees that looked like huge creatures, silhouetted by a moonlit backdrop. What was peaceful and picturesque in the daytime, was now the scene of every horror movie, as fog faintly wisped by.

The thickness of the dark would hide a multitude of things that ran from discovery. Dogs barked nervously at the sounds of dry grass crunching underneath anything that moved in the still night; and an ominous foretelling of what was to come in the next moments, was in the air to be grasped by those with a sixth sense. However, no one grasped it at this time of night, and therefore, the warning before destruction, was lost in the cool breeze that made the leaves flutter.

The girl in the shower had been chosen, she was alone in her huge home. Her parents were out of town, which meant she could do whatever she wanted, with whomever she wanted for the weekend. She didn't choose to be stared at by blood shot eyes that followed her every move throughout the house. She didn't choose the brutality that was coming her way. What she did choose, was the handsome young guy, armed with a six pack of beer tucked underneath his arm, and the Magnum condoms that he pushed deep into his back pocket.

He ensured that the condoms were there with one last pat of his jeans, before ringing the doorbell. Now the two of them would be stared at, as the assailant breathed heavily and angrily, contemplating how he would dispose of two bodies now.

Outside of the house, was still the frightening scene as before; fog that seemed to fall lower and thicker throughout the neighborhood, limiting visibility; dogs that all seemed to be howling in unison, like a pack of wolves baying to communicate a potential fresh kill; and an eerie stillness that enhanced the sounds of things that go bump in the night. Only this time, the night was disturbed by an unseen force that would ensure that evil prevailed. The masked man continued to watch the young couple as their playful giggles, turned into quiet, but intense foreplay. His rage helped to fuel his ambition for revenge.

Social Media told him what he needed to know about her; it helped him to determine that she was unworthy of a chance to live. She was always posting pictures with her friends at school, at church, at her part-time job, and with her parents. She was so beautiful and wholesome it seemed, as she posted affirmations, dream boards, relationship goals, and her, "Mr. Right." However, her posts in other forums, spoke of a different girl, who was not as wholesome. It spoke volumes of her unseen character. She touted her ability to make any man cum, in less than one minute; at least, that is what she told him, in just a few back and forth messages.

Without her realizing it, her killer sat next to her at Starbucks, as she met with friends one afternoon. Her hair smelled so sweet, and the way she turned and smiled at him, when he retrieved the scarf that she accidentally dropped, said it all. He would watch her from time to time, from a distance. Sometimes he would go to the mall, and watch her walk around with her friends; she never knew that he was there.

She never knew the numerous times that she walked right past him. Her head was usually buried in her cell phone, or she was engaged in some deep millennial conversation. He saw her, when no one else saw her, sneaking to have sex with guys, spreading her legs, exchanging STD's, and exchanging sexual conversations with a complete stranger. Whore!!!!

As he glared with pure hatred, his unquenched desire to kill was heightened tremendously. He opened the back door, which he had prepared for ingress the day before, and slid in undetected. The two lovers drowned out any discovery, by their loud sexual intensity. The blade was pulled from the jacket pocket, casting a reflection of a demon-like figure, with an animalistic narrowing of hunt in its eyes.

As he approached the couple, the reflection was soon marred by dark purple blood that obscured the pristine perfection of a mirrored blade. A beveled edge, sharpened with the precision to slice through 12 inches of solid beef in a single pass, was an easy challenge; as the blade slid easily through neck muscles, tendons, and bone that easily gave way; decapitating the young man, who fell over lifeless. The girl, frozen in fear, met her demise quickly, as the blade entered into her heart, and was pulled out, so that 20 more stabs to her torso could be effected.

The sight of blood was such a release of adrenaline that the killer could not stop laughing hysterically, as he rushed throughout the house drawing gang graffiti all over the walls with the warm blood that poured from his victims. After the gurgles of blood escaping the body ceased, and the wild merriment came to an abrupt halt, there was a dead silence, broken by a whistled tune that eerily pierced the air.

On a cold day warmed by a fireplace, with the smell of herbs and garlic on a roasting turkey, wafting through the air;

this tune would have been a welcomed accompaniment; but on a gloomy night, in the dead silence, as the smell of blood overtook the room, this was the most ill-omened adaptation of "Silent Night" ever rendered.

He slipped away from the house, just as quietly as he came, thrusting his body back into his vehicle. The moon and stars lit his path as he disappeared into the night, which was always a great cover for his transgressions. The dogs continued to howl nervously. The eyes of God looked on, as the killer proudly redeemed the failure of his escaped victim. The inception of this degeneracy came many years before, in an old country shack, where God was not welcome.

Chapter 3

The old dusty shack barely stood on its frame of rotting wood, and the cracked cement floor that made up its foundation. The holes in the wood beams allowed the cold brisk air to push through, chilling the very core of its inhabitants inside. However, the coldness of what took place inside, was even more chilling than the elements outside.

The wind whistled and howled angrily and insistently. For even Mother Nature stirs, when things aren't right. The occupants were Momma, and her frail little 7 year old daughter. They were poor, very poor. Sometimes dead squirrels were the top meal of the week, tenderized in a hot bowl of stew. Other times, they hit the jackpot when the men that frequented the old shack brought a sack of hamburgers, or left-over candy bars. This was the big pay-off for all of the hard work that the poor little frail girl had to put in. Momma worked too; she had loaned her daughter out to men ever since her daughter was two years old. Momma knew what it took to corral the young girl, and get her to do exactly what was necessary.

"You have to earn your keep around here," Momma said. "Now stop your crying, and make your uncle happy."

She never realized that she had so many uncles, and if they were the definition of uncles, then uncles weren't always kin. Why did the encounters all end the same way, and why did it have to hurt? However, at 7 years old, she learned what to expect. When she was not on her back, making grown men feel accomplished, she was beaten with anything laying around the house. It was great when Momma was drunk, because she would pass out, and the house would be quiet for a change, except for the rising wind that made its way through the seams of the shack.

Tonight was another night to pay dues for the battered girl. She already knew what to do, even though Momma barked orders to her anyway.

"Jane Doe, go and get in the shower, and get yourself pretty. Hurry up."

Momma thought it would be funny to name her daughter Jane Doe, to symbolize a girl with no identity, and no significance. Jane was brought into the world, unloved by her momma, and unknown by a man who took things by force.

Jane hurried up and showered, and then she climbed into a dirty king-size bed that her mother found, and drug into a backroom. The room was always cold and dark, no windows; lit by a small lamp that was missing a shade. Resting on the floor, it cast an orange glow that only extended a couple of feet; the remainder of the room did not benefit from its presence.

The room was dank and musty, with the smell of old cigarettes, sweat, semen, and lingering body odor.

Jane pulled the covers up to her neck, gripping the top of them until her knuckles turned white. She prepared to leave her body behind, and travel elsewhere in her mind. It was the only way to deal with the events this night would see.

She could hear her mother talking in the front room; a male voice chiming in, as he laughed loudly through heavy, phlegmy coughs. The voices seemed to be getting closer, approaching her. The frightened girl inched the covers up to her nose, seeking any protection from the simple toss that this animal would deliver when he was ready to have his way with her. Soon, it was proven that the tight grip on her covers would have no power, as the man pushed open the door, fell on the bed, and flung the cover off of her, in one fluid motion.

"Hello sweetheart," he said with a raspy, smoky voice.

His body odor was overpowering, and seeing his overweight, hairy body made her sick to her stomach, sparking a round of involuntary dry heaves.

"How about a little kiss sweetheart?"

He did not wait for a response, as he quickly overtook her, forcing his tongue into her mouth, muffling her screams.

"Don't hurt her bad in there, she's quality merchandise," she heard her momma yell from beyond the door.

She felt thick knobby fingers forcing their way into her, pulling at her flesh, penetrating her tiny womb and releasing a stream of blood that trickled onto his fingers. His grunts and groans seemed to get louder, as his excitement mounted at the sight of the blood. She blacked out, and when she came to, there was only the remainder of his release. She lay in a sticky, bloody mess, her body sore, and she was unable to move without pain. Momma came to the door; not to console her daughter.

"Get in the shower, and get something to eat. You got comp'ny coming in an hour."

By the time of Jane's 14th birthday, she had more sex partners than anyone could have thought possible. However, by this time, she became a well-oiled machine, she was not in control of her body, that part of her body did not even belong to her anymore. It was inhabited by one of her other personalities she developed specifically just to deal with sex. This personality was good at it, and even loved it. She had something that men wanted badly, and she could bargain for anything that she wanted with that power.

She didn't realize that she had no real power, for even that was controlled by Momma.

However, her momma died just a few days after her birthday. Jane didn't cry, but immediately grabbed a rusty shovel and began digging. It took all day to make a grave large enough to bury the body, but she worked non-stop for hours just to get her mother's sick twisted body, into the cold hard earth.

"I hope I get her a little closer to Hell," she thought with delight. At this moment, Jane felt more peace than she had ever before.

However, the quietness became more than she could bear. Her idea of peace was to have a huge sex and drug-filled party to celebrate the end of a reign. She invited some of the men that Momma kept on a piece of paper; and they came to the shack willingly with no questions asked. However, things didn't go as planned, and she ended up as the victim of a gang bang that would be videotaped, a house that would be trashed, and an overdose that almost cost her life.

She recovered in the hospital, but found herself in the custody of child protective services upon her recovery. The shock and confusion of her surroundings was overwhelming. She had never been anywhere beyond that shack. She never attended school, she never went to a doctor's appointment, and she never went to town. Who would even care enough to get her to a hospital? Questions and investigations soon followed, as they wanted to know the whereabouts of her mother. Her unwillingness to answer, or cooperate, made her more of a suspect than a victim.

After her recovery, she was placed in a youth transitional center while investigations ensued. It wasn't long before she solicited help from some cohorts from the center, and she was able to escape. She ran away to the biggest state that she could find, Texas. She heard that everything was bigger in Texas, and no one would look for her there, even better, no one could find her if they tried. However, Jane would soon realize that no matter how far away she went, or where she ended up in life, her mother's rule would always be over her. Jane would respond to it, just like she was trained to do.

What Jane did not know is that she was born into a satanic child prostitution ring. Jane was abused mentally, physically, and sexually, in such a way that the traumatic effects allowed her mind to be controlled. The various personalities that Jane developed to cope with the horrific situations in her life were influences created by her environment, her abuse, her abusers, and the demonic strongholds in her life. Jane never knew what made her different, she did whatever it took to survive, even if it took multiple personalities to get through it. For some, this manifested as a natural defense mechanism, but in Jane's case, it was a true satanic hold. Thousands upon thousands of demons were imparted into her womb, each time that she had sex with a different man while under her mother's control. These demons would now be passed to every man with whom she had sex.

Their manifestations would be far-reaching, creating legions of powerful forces that the men passed on to their spouses, or sexual partners. However, her purpose did not stop there. A greater manifestation would come from her very own loins, to continue the spread of evil, and continue Maniac's desire for carnage and death.

For at a certain time and place, a trigger would cause her to continue in the deeds that Satan, and his followers wanted her to participate in. She never knew the evil plan for her life since her birth. Jane's mother, Catherine, was used to lure men to have sex with her daughter. These men came from all walks of life. Some of them were prestigious and affluent, some were petty drug dealers, and some where married men, with children of their own. It didn't matter their status, they were all participants in terrible sex acts against a child, worthy of the death penalty; but in a world where these acts were prevalent, the true crime was the sound of silence.

Chapter 4

In the old rickety shack many years before Jane was born, there brewed an evil assignment that would birth an instrument of death. Jane Doe was born to Catherine, and Catherine was the product of evil beginnings. Catherine knew her purpose in life, and she knew it well, even at a young age.

Her own life was spared, even though she wished at times that her life was taken away from her. Incest was a common occurrence in the household; her daddy, uncles, and even granddaddy, always seemed to find their way into her bed, and deep into her body. Catherine's momma died when she was just 13, this is when the sex increased; for before then, it was only during deep nights when daddy would slip away from the bed that he shared with his wife, to enter the room where she lay. She would try to pretend that she was sleep, but this never stopped his advances.

"Give poppa some of the fun stuff," he would say, but it was never fun.

She would lay there as he entered her from behind, staring over at the next bed where her two little sisters lay; squeezing their eyes shut, pretending to be asleep. She would try not to make a sound, as her poppa's thrusts got harder, shaking the bed until it squeaked rhythmically. Soon the sounds could not be contained, and she would let out moans that were confusing; as she didn't understand if she was moaning and crying out for the pain, or the eventual pleasure.

Poppa would get up, stumble over to the other bed, and rub on the other two girls, promising that they would get their turn next time, as he bent over to kiss them, while tucking his emptied, flaccid penis back into his Long Johns. It was never enough for Poppa.

He worked with some type of government agency, and would be gone for long periods of time. When he was at home, he would come and go from the house; and would sometimes come home late, and go straight to his old horse barn in the back, staying out there for hours. Catherine's momma knew better than to ask him about his business.

She was just happy that he wasn't slapping her to unconsciousness the way he usually did; even though he knew that she had cancer. This never stopped him from delivering all out beatings, which would break the poor woman's body down further. He tried to cure her with injections that he brought home from work, and kept in a black bag.

No one ever went near his black bag, they all learned the hard way, when it resulted in a tyrant from Poppa. However, the injections didn't work; and so, she became useless to him.

She was just there to watch the three girls while he was away on business; he didn't need her for anything else, because all of his other needs seemed to be met by his daughters, and countless others.

Poppa had friends, lots of friends. Some of them were men that Catherine knew from their town, some were his co-workers, and some were relatives. They always seemed to come around when Poppa was home. They would meet in the barn. Catherine knew a lot about them, because she would have to go to the barn sometimes.

It was there that she would meet other children; but these were not kids that she was ever allowed to befriend, they were there in the same zombie-like state that Catherine was in most of the time. The men would gather around her while she lay on a table, her head spinning out of control. She couldn't make out faces after a while, just blurred figures of what she thought were people. The men would take turns having sex with her; they would hurt her physically sometimes, by slicing at her flesh with knives, or poking her with hot metal rods.

She would lay there unable to control her thought processes, unable to fight, unable to think straight. She could hear the loud shrieks and chants of the men, and the loud cries from the children in the barn, it just seemed like lots of vociferous noises. She swore that she saw the devil one time, but since she was really unsure of what she saw, she figured it was all just one distorted mind trip.

By the time she woke up, she would be in her bed, with clear thoughts, and vague memories. She never asked Poppa about them, because she feared any type of conversation with him, would bring unwanted attention to her; which would eventually mean unwelcomed advances for sex. She tried to stay out of his line of sight, as much as possible. So she was glad when he went away for work.

She was always relieved when he was away; but unfortunately, she was left with the nightmares that were impregnated in her psyche when he wasn't there. She had nightmares about the babies and other children that she saw. She would often dream of lots of blood; either blood spilling, blood pouring, blood being drank; or some other bizarre act with blood. She had nightmares about creatures with the most hideous faces, or ghosts that would pass through rooms of her house, she was terrified.

Her momma was of no comfort and stayed in bed most of the time; and the girls tended to her, as her health began to fade. She wasn't much of a caring mother anyway. Even before her health began to fade, she always walked around in a stupor, sliding her feet on the floor, instead of picking them up. Her hair was always a mess, and she was always sleepy, and this is the way that Catherine remembered her. Poppa would come home and give her injections to help her cope, but this only made her symptoms worse, and she would lay in bed catatonic, leaving Catherine and her sisters to fend for themselves. The girls didn't go to school, and no one bothered the family to inquire about their absence from society.

When Poppa was home, sometimes he would beat momma right in front of the girls. He would forbid the girls to cry, or hide their faces; if they did, he would beat them as well. Momma would be slung around like a rag doll, flying all over the house until he got tired. The girls were not allowed to touch her. They could not console her, and when she finally died, it was a relief; because they would not have to be subjected to listening to Momma beg and cry in agony, as new bruises and cuts were put on top of old ones, which had not yet healed.

Catherine's relief was short lived though, as she became the woman of the house at just thirteen years of age. After she got her period, the sexual abuse was much more frequent, and so were the beatings and torture, but Catherine was strong, and withstood every bit of torture that she was subjected to; and this earned her status over the other children that were brought to the barn. She saw kids of all races and all ages, but she never knew where they came from, only that they were all scared, and they would have to go through something traumatic at the hands of the men, who frequented the barn.

Catherine's strong-will, helped her to be callus and ignore begs, screams, and cries from the victims. She helped Poppa and the others, to hold the children down while they were tortured in unspeakable ways. Catherine would usually be in a dream or trance-like state, and it was during those times in the barn, that she would see things that did not seem like reality. It made her question her sanity, and made her wonder what was real, and what was a figment of her imagination. She stayed in a state of confusion, as she watched men in a large circle, ask for power from an invisible source that they seemed to pray to.

Suddenly, creatures and devils would appear, and they appeared to enter the men, and take over their bodies. Causing the men to act erratically, as their evil senses became heightened. They would cut themselves, or act in a violent sexual nature, or stand with their arms raised, convulsing wildly, as they invoked greater power and knowledge.

Sometimes, a devil-like figure, or apparition would talk directly to Catherine directing her what to do next, and she obeyed. She knew that she must prove her worthiness to the group, and her loyalty was tested, when Poppa brought her younger sisters to the circle. Like innocent lambs brought to slaughter, the two girls gave no resistance, as they were placed on a wooden table. The girl's innocence was a sweet smell in the nostrils of such vile men who preyed upon the girls. The men relied upon the girls to bring more demons through open portals, who anticipated the sacrifice. Catherine vaguely remembered holding the knife that entered the hearts of her sisters. She remembered having a nightmare about blood again, but she did not remember anything else. She dreamed that the blood was mixed with animal blood, which would later be reintroduced into a newborn baby.

When Catherine woke up the next morning, the house was quiet; her sisters were gone, and never seen or heard from again, it was just Catherine and Poppa. Catherine was now the overseer of the children that Poppa, and the other men from the circle, would bring to the house. Catherine was directed by a demonic influence, who would tell her what to do. She seemed to be able to sense what the children would be used for. She would help cultivate their strengths, and eliminate those who were weak, or could not handle the assignments given to them.

Some of the children were killed; blood drained, and flesh eaten by the men, or by the other children, at the direction of the animalistic men of the group. Some were trained, and their minds were controlled to be used like Manchurian Candidates, for a later date for some type of agenda, like a mass killing, shooting spree, assassination, to spread diseases, or to push drugs into their neighborhoods.

Everyone there had an assignment, and a purpose for being there. They were kidnapped, drugged, and held against their will, and the families of the missing would often never see them again. No bodies to be buried, no closure, no good byes, the sadness of the activities that took place was unsettling and despicable.

Catherine was chosen to continue a bloodline that the evil forces in Hell wanted birthed into the world. She proved that she was strong enough, and callus enough to carry out any assignment that was given to her. Many of her drug-induced rapes produced offspring, but Catherine would never see the children that she gave birth to, and the kids that were brought to the house came and went, and she never saw them again either. For years these horrific events took place, until one day Poppa left, and did not come back home. One of her uncles came to the house after a few weeks had passed, to tell her of his demise in a car accident.

Catherine was alone, until she discovered that she was with child. It would be so easy for Catherine to simply snuff the child out at birth, but she was directed by the demons that seemed to possess her life, to keep the child, a baby girl that she would call Jane Doe.

She would use Jane Doe as her new extension for sex, which she no longer had to take part in. Men would come around just to have sex with the young girl, who Catherine never showed any love for. Just like her father taught her, she would teach Jane how to block out her feelings, and conjure spirits inside of her to be used for whatever the spirits needed her for.

And so, all of the demons that imparted themselves in Catherine's womb entered into Jane, and as Jane was penetrated again and again by men from all walks of life as part of one of the biggest child prostitution rings in the state, she was filled with evil, hate, self-destruction, and demons that she could spread back to the men that she had sex with.

Although Jane Doe moved from the state to start a new life, the demons that were a part of her life did not stay behind, they moved with her, and the generational curse followed her to her new destination. The influences that she thought that she saw buried the day that she put her mother into ground, were right there in Texas when she arrived. There were still bad people in every state, there were still satanic influences everywhere, and there would be heinous events that were affecting people, no matter where she would have decided to run.

Jane lived on the streets for a couple of years, barely getting by. Her conditions in that rickety shack prepared her for hard days ahead. These days were no better, but definitely no worse. She did the only thing that she knew how to do and what she did best, she had sex. She was still programmed to hear those fateful words from her momma,

"Go get in the shower, and get yourself cleaned up, you have comp'ny."

Jane knew that when she heard those words in her head, that it was show time. Time for her sexual personalities to emerge and take over. Her showers were methodical and sensual, as she prepared herself to be alluring, and enticing to the men that would visit. There was a personality that came forth known as Pria; it was the personality that helped her not to be afraid; but accepting of her fate. Pria would fully emerge at the moment that Jane prepared for sex with one of her suitors. Pria was the strong one, and controlled the other personalities. It would assign the demons and new personalities, which passed quickly through the shaft of a throbbing dick; that penetrated, and emptied into Jane's womb; spilling into her, and imparting themselves deep into the crowded walls of her sexual anteroom.

More personalities would emerge and help her during these periods as well. "Danas" was a personality that helped her to fly away to some place more beautiful, occupy her mind, so that she was unaware of the abuse that her body was taking, during uncaring, and unflinching sexual torture. Sometimes, the personality known as "Lilli," helped her to be really good at sex; this personality was a man and a woman intertwined. It was wild and bold and gave the men mind-blowing orgasms that lasted for extended periods, like an addictive drug. Many more personalities had their role, and the transfer of demonic spirits back and forth between herself and her sex partners created a powerful and dangerous possession that could not be contained.

Jane cleaned herself up in seedy hotels, and awaited her many lovers underneath the floral print comforters, that had not been updated since the 70's. The same ritual she had always known made her successful at delivering sex, which seemed to call men like a beacon in the night. Only this time, she got to keep the money that was given to her.

When she was home with her Momma, during her coming of age years, she never saw money. She was rewarded with drugs; hallucinogens that would help her go even further into her consciousness. The drugs helped her forget the pain and misery, and go into an altered state that allowed her to be a willing participant. In this state, she was acquainted with Pria, who made everything tolerable.

Now, she realized that sex gained her money, and money provided her the things that she never really had regularly, like food, jewelry, and clothes. She never knew that during those years at home, the money paid for her abortions, treatments for STD's, and more drugs for her and Momma to utilize.

Not every one of her pregnancies resulted in abortion; sometimes her babies were allowed to be born, but they were taken away from her immediately, before she could protest. Producing babies was a bigger payday for Momma. There was use for the babies that were born, and Momma helped determine if the baby would live or die. If the baby was healthy and strong, it could be used for an assignment later, and it lived.

However, if it was not worthy of life, its body parts were used, sold, or sacrificed in some type of ritual. Jane never knew that these deeds unfolded in her life. She was too high, or mind-altered to realize that she was a cash cow, a breeder, and a puppet.

What she did know now, was that she was 17 and pregnant, and there was no one to take that problem away. She knew in her heart her purpose was to raise this little inconvenience. Jane did whatever she had to do to survive on those tough Houston streets, and when she ran into a prominent man in the community, she thought that help was within reach; until he impregnated her, and left her to the streets, threatening her if she told anyone.

Her pregnancy resulted in the birth of a son, John; John Doe. All of the demons, that were lying dormant like a sleeper cell in her womb, were more than anxious to attach themselves to the child; giving him the unfortunate burden of carrying them now. Jane hated him, he was an encumbrance to her that slowed her down. It, as she referred to him as; always wanted to eat, and she had to provide things that she never even knew how to provide for herself such as shelter, clothing, and food. The next year was even harder for her, with John in her life. She and John went from couch to couch, sometimes at stranger's houses, until they wanted her out, and then she would go to shelters. Sometimes they would curl up next to a business that had a heater, so that they could feel the warm air drifting off its blazing red coils.

By the time Jane was 18, she knew what she was destined to do. She knew sex very well, and she became good at orchestrating the sex of the other young girls living in the streets. Jane recruited other girls, and sent them out as well, so that she did not have to take part in the sadistic activities as much as she had before; however, the amount of sex that she had to put out never diminished. Also, with the burden of a child always around, she realized that she did not want to be responsible for anyone else.

She became her momma reincarnate. She was without remorse; making money was the only thing on her mind. However, the lifestyle was a dangerous one, and for the next seven years, John had to be right there in the heart of the danger. He watched men come and go from the hotel rooms; oftentimes, having sex with his mom right in front of him.

He watched his mother experience beatings that left her bloody and busted. He watched her do horrible things to the other girls who were not compliant with the sexual requests of the johns. John was never allowed to cry or feel sorry for his mom; she was a proud, mean woman. She would stare at him through blackened eyes and tell him to shut up whenever he whimpered or cried.

After going through tough times and homelessness, with a young child; she returned to the man that put her in that position, begging for his mercy. He gave her an apartment with the stipulation that she would have sex with men of all walks of life; that paid the money for services rendered. The apartment didn't serve as a haven for her or John. Horrific and heinous acts continued to take place in the tiny apartment, which John and his mother shared with every other drug lord, pedophile, and low-life that came in and out whenever they pleased.

Jane's own abuse was projected onto the young boy, as she abused him, and allowed the men that frequented her apartment to abuse him. She laughed wildly every time John winced. He was once hit so hard that his body flew through the air and slammed into the wall. He hit the wall head first, which caused him to black out. He ended up laying there for hours until he regained consciousness; then he simply crawled to the couch and cried himself to sleep.

Sometimes, to keep John occupied during one of her sex and drug binges, she would put a DVD in the player, which played the same cartoon repeatedly; the song, "Silent Night," played non-stop. It played in a loop, and John would sit on the couch for hours watching it. Sometimes he raised the volume to cover the loud screams for mercy he heard coming from the back bedroom where his mother was being tortured. He sat with his little hands clenched in his lap, and his jaw tight. Urine would pool beneath him, and tears would stream down his cheeks but he knew that he dared not move from that couch.

So, oftentimes, he would sit there all day with no food, sores forming on his rear end from the urine, and the lack of movement. Eventually, his mother would come out of her room, after periods of unconsciousness, and tell John to get in the tub, as she cursed him out for urinating or defecating on himself. He did not talk back, and soon he did not talk at all, for talking brought negative consequences. He whistled "Silent

Night," when he felt anxious or stressed, to cope with what he was going through.

John was often the victim of heinous torture and abuse. He was once caught sucking his thumb after witnessing three men in his apartment hit a young girl in the head repeatedly until she fell over, and began to convulse. His momma grabbed his chin, and looked him squarely in the eyes and said,

"Whores don't deserve to live, sometimes they are more useful dead."

She shoved John's head back into the couch that he was sitting on. John immediately pulled his legs in, and got into a fetal position, as he began to suck his thumb.

"I will break that little thumb of yours, stop acting like a baby," and with that, his momma yanked John's thumb out of his mouth, and bent it backwards, almost breaking it.

One of the men chimed in,

"You better not cry, you little bastard," and he turned to Jane.

"You should let us have him for a day or so, we will make a little soldier out of him, so that he will be good for something."

John was dragged to a closet, and locked inside until the next day. He blacked out, and was in and out of consciousness throughout the night. When he came to, the body of the young girl that was hit over the head was lying next to him. His mother opened the door, peering down at John, who was paralyzed with fear.

"What did you do? Did you kill that girl John?" she asked sternly.

John stayed silent. He didn't think that he did it, but he was unsure.

"Now I have to get this mess cleaned up, go sit on the couch," she said.

John quickly ran over to his designated spot on the couch, and began rocking back and forth, confused, as the DVD began playing "Silent Night" loudly. Mother took the body to the bathroom, and began cutting the little girl up, and bagging up various parts of her body. Men came by moments later to take the parts away as John sat frozen in fear, his eyes glued to the television.

"Silent Night, Holy Night, All is Calm, All is Bright."

This song only meant one thing when it was played, something terrible was going to happen. Although total chaos was ensuing, the soft melodies of this song brought solace to a horrific situation, making it a little more bearable. John proved to be a strong little soldier indeed. He kept quiet, didn't cry, and his heart and mind became trained to accept the inevitable.

His mother, on the other hand, was deteriorating, and even the familiar tune of "Silent Night" was not able to cover the sights and sounds of what was taking place. His mother continued to be slapped around by men, and she began to degrade herself; crawling around, picking up pieces of crack from the carpet to smoke. She performed oral sex right in front of the couch, impeding John's view of his cartoon, so that she could earn a little more crack. John simply moved around a little bit, annoyed that she was blocking the view, even though the cartoon was ingrained in his head.

Jane was tired of the sex and abuse that she experienced her entire life. In her apartment, many atrocities took place; young women were held there against their will, until they were sold off, killed, or taken away. Jane was callous to the occurrences, and John was as well. This wasn't the lifestyle that she wanted to continue for the rest of her life, but saw no way out, it was the only life she had ever known.

One morning, John awakened to the sound of his familiar cartoon, as he rubbed his eyes looking for his momma. He didn't have to search far, as he saw her legs halfway out of the door of her bedroom. This came as no surprise, as he often found her on the floor, after a wild night of sex and drugs; but this time she was cold and stiff. She had a needle sticking out from between her toes, the last place that she could shoot up.

She made the decision to end her own curse, so she mixed several drugs together; snorting, swallowing, and injecting, everything that she could get a hold of, so that she could die. However, the curse did not end with her, because now John had to live with the sins of his generation. This was her final selfish act, as she left the young child sitting on the couch to face whatever fate he had coming to him in his life.

John carried on, leaving her body right there for days as he watched his DVD. Eventually, he ate whatever he could find in the fridge, and drank leftover beer in overturned cans on the floor, while constantly ignoring knocks on the door from men looking for sex, or confinement for their captives. Detained victims that momma housed in a back room, under lock and key.

The smell didn't bother John, but apparently, it bothered everyone else, because a police officer finally kicked the door down, finding John sitting on the couch watching his DVD, with his decomposing mother; her flesh rotting, and sloughing off into a pool of viscous body fluids. The officer stumbled out of the apartment throwing up, but he returned with tears in his eyes, scooping John up, embracing him tightly, and carrying him outside.

Chapter 5

John swallowed another cup of coffee, as he reminisced about that fateful day that he was rescued by his adoptive father, Officer Kyle Bigsby. He finally had an identity and was no longer a John Doe; John Bigsby was a name he was proud to possess. He began to whistle his favorite tune, "Silent Night," as he poured yet another cup of coffee, making this one his third in less than 30 minutes.

He surfed the internet briefly, as memories of his childhood flooded his head. There was never a quiet moment in John's head. He wished that all the voices and memories would go away and leave him be, but they wouldn't. It was like it was yesterday that he could hear his dad's voice when he was just 10 years old.

Beyond his years of living with his uncaring mom, was his life with his adoptive father; the first person that made his life seem easier. Officer Bigsby bonded with John instantly after the rescue. He was a single man that always wanted a son, but being a police officer kept him plenty busy; too busy for a social life. However, after the rescue, John was allowed to live with the police officer, who was more than willing to rear John as his protégé.

"John, eat your oatmeal buddy, we have to get going. Your old man is being promoted today!" John remembered his dad proclaiming proudly.

John could remember gulping down his third cup of orange juice, as he continued to stare into space. Most of those days, his mind was filled with chaos, thoughts, and voices that overwhelmed his brain; although, the world outside of his mind moved in quiet, perfect harmony. Sometimes the voices that were the loudest, and clearest, were the meanest. It was hard for John to distinguish what was real, and what were really the voices initiated by the "Dark Man." The Dark Man used to just come when John closed his eyes to go to sleep, so that he could follow John into his dreams; but now it would materialize into a living being, that apparently, only John could see.

He was John's imaginary friend; he was a protector. When John had nightmares, or the voices in his head got louder and louder, Dark Man would yell, and make everything quiet again, so that only his voice was distinctly heard. Dark Man came around more often at that time in John's life.

He even sat at the table with John on this particular day and peered across the table with an evil blank stare at John's father, who was oblivious to the fact that his son was joined by such sinister company.

"Buddy, please don't do this today, we have to get going. I don't want to be late." Officer Bigsby spoke louder this time.

John took another swallow of orange juice and pushed his bowl to the empty place setting to his left.

"You eat it," he said, talking to the dark man who never broke his gaze at Officer Bigsby.

Officer Bigsby grabbed his gun belt, and his duffle bag that sat in the chair next to him.

"Let's go," he said, "Now!"

John wiped his mouth with his balled-up napkin, and threw it on the floor, as he raced upstairs to get his backpack that he left on his bed. As he hurried back downstairs, he could see Dark Man still sitting in the same spot; unflinching as he followed Officer Bigsby around the kitchen, with only his bulged out yellow eyes glowing like headlights.

"You leave him alone," John said.

"Leave who alone?" Officer Bigsby asked, obviously upset at his son's behavior on this important morning.

"Go away," John said insistent, yet fearful; Dark Man disappeared.

Officer Bigsby's promotion was at the forefront of his mind. He didn't have time to deal with the voices that constantly plagued John. He knew what he signed up for, taking on a child with so much trauma; but today was his day to be named detective, and he didn't want anything to spoil this moment. John climbed into the police cruiser, sliding in as close to his dad as he could get; which wasn't close, with all of the gadgets that were meant to uncomplicate a busy police officer's life. Officer Bigsby cranked the car and looked over at his son with a smile.

"One day son, you will be like your old man. People will respect you, and appreciate you for all of your hard work. Do something important in life, no matter what you decide to do. Make sure that you make your mark on the world, ok!"

John looked into his dad's eyes, unsure of what he truly meant. Never in his wildest dreams, did he think that his mark on the world would be as impactful as being a serial killer with the power to elude discovery and capture. Never in his wildest dreams did he think that, years later, he would lose the one person that cared for him.

It was Dark Man, not John that took his father away. John never would have taken the life of the only person that he ever cared about; but Dark Man hated his father Kyle. Officer Bigsby led by Godly principles. He prayed for John's well-being, mind, body, and soul; and he made John pray daily. Dark Man was opposite, and wanted things handled by violence and force; he plagued John's thoughts every time John tried to pray. He made the voices louder, and he terrorized John's dreams.

John was convinced that Dark Man had incapacitated him so that he could carry out the cruel assignment of murdering his dad. When John woke up, he found his dad unresponsive. The coroner said that it was a heart attack, but John knew who was responsible. It was Dark Man that gave him the barium acetate that caused his untimely death.

Dark Man glared at John, who knew better than to cry or show pain for a loss of life. It didn't sit right with John, but his early predisposition for psychopathy, didn't allow him to mourn or feel remorse for very long, if at all. John picked up the telephone and made the call that would bring every detective, police officer, and EMT to the house. One of their own was gone, and it was a tragic loss for the entire department. They consoled John and vowed from that day forward to always take care of him. He was now a brother to the entire police family, and this outpouring of support gave John the confidence to achieve anything that he wanted, especially with the loyalty and protection of his new family.

Therefore, when John sat before the board to become a police officer himself, and later a detective, it was a no-brainer to accept him into the tight-knit family of blue. He proved to be a great police officer just like his dad and stepped right into his shoes without a hitch. The police department did not hesitate in promoting John to the position; and John did not let their decision to promote him be one of regret. John was great at everything that he did. He didn't speak very much, but he was smart, and he was good. The tune "Silent Night," always echoed down the halls, and throughout the police department, even when it was not Christmas time.

John snapped out of his reminiscence, as he unfolded a stick of gum, and shoved into his mouth. He grabbed his suit jacket and headed to his assignment as lead detective on yet another murder case. John was familiar with the case; he knew the scene before he got there. He slowly backed out of his driveway, gripping his steering wheel tightly as his jaws clenched, anticipating a stressful day.

This part of Texas had seen its share of murder and mayhem. Blood ran down the streets and seeped into the Earth. It trickled into storm drains, lakes and rivers, across pavements, and sometimes was splattered on walls. There was never a dull moment in the biggest city in Texas. For every person that died, a child was born, for every person that moved away, there were 100 people or more to replace them. Houston was crowded, and for all the death that occurred almost daily, it still did not put a dent in the population, with its vast numbers of people who resided there. Homicide detectives stayed busy with their open cases; only to have unsolved murders, and cold cases to continue to stack up, inundating the detectives who put in more than their fair share of work. It was daunting, tiring, and sad; but bringing closure to the families, loved ones, and friends of the deceased, made it worth it all. Nothing felt more fulfilling than writing "solved" on the board of open cases.

A feeling that John got the opportunity to be a part of countless times. The fact that he could solve murders so quickly made him the best. It was like he had a sixth sense for catching the perpetrators of these crimes. He was always hailed a hero for bringing closure to grieving families. It was the least he could do, he couldn't bring them back. At least in the minds of the family, justice was served to the killer. John enjoyed the success and praise that he received from solving these unsolvable cases. He always needed the assurance that he was good at something; that he was smart, or that he was successful.

Failure was not an option when John was young, his mother took that option off the table for him, when he was just a young boy. He peeked into a back bedroom once, when he heard some girls crying out for help. The young girls were bound with rope, and they were lying head to foot on the bed, naked. When one of the girls spotted John, she screamed for help, sparking the attention of his mother, who had stepped away for a moment to retrieve needles and syringes from the bathroom.

When she saw John standing with the door open to the forbidden room which she had warned him numerous times not to go into, she slapped John so hard his jaw shifted. He saw stars and temporarily lost his hearing.

"What happens when we screw up John?" she asked, after taping the girls' mouths shut and injecting them, incapacitating them instantly.

John did not answer her, and began to urinate on himself as his body shook.

"Oh, now we can't talk, and we pee on ourselves like a baby," she taunted. "What a little loser you are. They could have got away John, and we would have been in so much trouble. How could you be such a failure?" she insisted. "Loser, loser, loser," she said, each time she pushed him into the wall, knocking his head into it. "Go to the closet! Since you like to be nosy and look at things that you are not supposed to, you will look at the darkness. Stand up in there, and if I catch you sitting down or laying down, I will burn you. Do you understand?!!!"

John's mother threw him into the closet, he tripped and fell to the floor, but he quickly stood up, staring into the darkness. He wasn't alone for long, as he was further tormented by the demons that laughed at him and mocked him; the fear and the torment bringing him to the brink of insanity. He didn't know how long he stood in there. Hours, days, a week? It was long enough to get the point across. Never fail again.

Any slip ups now sparked mania in him. John could not afford to get caught, he was already disappointed in himself; for he felt he was spiraling out of control and making poor decisions after the girl got away from him that night. He beat himself up each day and decided to kill daily to rectify the situation.

"I can't let anyone be found again," he thought as he slapped himself for being sloppy enough to allow one to get away.

The detective arrived at the location that looked so different in the daytime. Yellow caution tape already decorated the area where the bodies were located, ensuring a crowd of inquisitive on-lookers. Flies and the stench of rot, wafted from the open door. In the midst of all the chaos, lay a young girl; her long hair caked with blood, slightly covering her face, revealing one of her partially opened eyes. Her arms were outstretched, legs apart, revealing that she had been unable to pull her limbs in to protect her vital organs.

"What happened here?" John asked, though he already knew.

"Well, just upon our initial observation, it appears that she was stabbed in the chest and torso numerous times. It looks like someone hated this girl."

The young police officer continued to talk as John gazed upon the girl, lost in his own thoughts.

The sight of the deceased girl lying there reminded him of his mother. He could still see her body lying on the floor. His thoughts were not of sadness, but at how death brought about a certain peace and quiet that he found pleasant. A slight smile peeled across John's face, making those around him take notice.

"Detective, what are your thoughts on this one?" another detective said, breaking into John's deep thoughts.

"Any evidence left behind for us?" John asked, looking around the scene carefully.

"The killer wrote on the walls with their blood," the other detective stated, as he pointed to the numerous places where bloody words cascaded down the wall and dried ominously. "Hopefully, we will get some good prints off of them, or if we are lucky enough, the killer cut his hand, and left some of his blood up there for us."

John hid the anger that he felt for his foolishness as he stepped across the scene carefully to observe the other body. As he squatted for a closer look, he quickly checked his own hands for cuts, but was interrupted as other detectives stepped in to make their observations.

"Look at this," one of the detectives motioned to the ground. "I think we may have a lucky break, gum."

John quickly went over to the area; his heart racing. "I'll take it and get it processed." John said reaching down for it.

"What are you doing John?" The detective looked confused at John's inconsistent behavior.

"I'm sorry, I just hate it when we lose kids, especially when it's this gruesome. There is a head on the floor, away from the body, for Christ's sake."

"I don't know who you are right now," the detective said, with a deepening frown.

"I guess I'm a little off my game," John said, as he took the gum, and placed it in a bag, hiding it, as he continued to walk through the scene. "I'm going to step outside, and get a little air. You guys continue, I'll be right back."

"Are you ok Biggs?" the other detective asked.

"I'm fine!" John began to feel the anger in his throat, as the words came out harshly.

John looked over at the girl again, who still looked just as beautiful to him in her state of rigor mortis as she did when the blood flowed through her rosy cheeks, when she smiled at him. He felt the blood pulse through his cock, making it swell, as the twisted scene turned him on. He hurriedly retreated outside, so as not to bring attention to the bulge. He took off his suit jacket, folding it neatly over his arm to create the curtain effect needed to hide his perverseness. He was met by a crowd of people pressing in as close as they could before breaking the caution tape that held them at bay. Police officers did their best to control the mob. News crews converged on the scene as reporters jumped out of vehicles, and set up quickly to be the first to report the tragedy.

John looked beyond the chaos, across the street, at the row of trees that graced the neighborhood with their majestic foliage. He noticed his imaginary friend that followed him from his childhood, staring at him. The tall, slender, dark figure had a gait of disappointment, as its erratic breathing made its shoulders rise and fall; his fiendish yellow eyes protruding as he stared a hole through John's soul.

It suddenly disappeared, though no one else saw it anyway. John turned away frustrated, as he walked towards his car, leaving the coroners, detectives, and police officers to their work. He felt the veins in his head gorge and throb, causing a splitting headache that almost incapacitated him.

John climbed into his vehicle and stared out of his driver-side window; scanning the Thomas Kincaid backdrop that became an early grave for an undeserving girl, and her unsuspecting partner. His eyes darted rapidly, as he searched for the dark figure that he had seen before. He searched with childlike anticipation for confirmation that his deeds were seen and approved.

His childhood haunted him, reminding him that he had better do things right, or there would be hell to pay. John drove away from the scene, even though he was the lead on this case. As usual, no one questioned him; they continued to process the scene, only pausing to see his brake lights at the stop sign, at the end of the street. The car quietly drove away; the killer, looking ahead into the sunlit day whistling his favorite tune.

Chapter 6

Killing was a way to satisfy the numerous voices that plagued his brain, and it made Dark Man stay out of his consciousness. If he did not kill exactly the way Dark Man told him to, he would be punished with horrific nightmares, plagued with the most excruciating migraines one could imagine.

To make matters worse, during moments of intense pain and fear, he heard thousands of voices, all talking at different times; yelling, screaming, and piercing his brain with a horrendous crescendo. He always did what he was told, and Dark Man would either nod with pleasure; or with a look of disdain, he would shake his head slowly, scowling at John's failure.

Disappointment was a quality, that of which John never wanted to be guilty. His idea of success was a distorted view of murder and mayhem, and the ability to go undetected. Getting caught was never a worry before, but for the first time since his father's death, John's inattentiveness to his craft made him question his ability to remain undetectable.

John Bigsby loved to kill for the ecstasy, and exhilaration that it brought to him whenever he did it. John's brain rarely went a moment without his synapses firing rapidly. He always stayed two steps ahead of everyone else. The information gathered today would help him with important steps days, and sometimes weeks away.

He hunted people like a ravenous wolf, strategically lurking in the shadows, and patiently waiting for signs of vulnerability from his prey. He usually waited a while before he killed again, and he made sure to do this so he could plan carefully who he killed, how he killed, and where he killed. He had to be sure that each step led to the other, perfectly, just the way that Dark Man orchestrated it. However, his desires to kill burned hot within him, and before this fresh kill could turn cold, he was ready to do it again.

John understood he was not a good man, this was a fact that he just learned to accept. Even when his father would tell him that he was good, and how God would bless him with greatness someday, John knew in his heart that he was not worthy of anything good; because his heart would harden at the mention of God, whom he felt had deserted him, leaving him at the hands of a mean and callous mother.

His mama made sure that he knew that he was a terrible, good-for-nothing boy with evil in his heart. So, John learned to accept the evil persona his mother gave him. He accepted whatever momma told him, and even though his father worked hard to encourage and uplift his damaged son; the evil outweighed the good in John's world. So evil, deceit, and anger came naturally for him. Therefore, positive, pure, honest and Godly things were foreign and unnatural, and made John nervous enough to sacrilegiously whistle a tune meant for peace, but used for the serenity it provided when invoking evil and death.

***

With police authority came power, but police power given to a psychopath was a dangerous combination. A psychopathic police officer, who was also a serial killer, was a dynamic from the very pits of Hell. John was able to manipulate situations in his favor, he was able to manipulate people to benefit his agendas, and this is precisely what he did. He had access to evidence, drugs, addresses, phone numbers, even bank accounts if he really wanted it. The demonic influence that consumed John helped him to be one of the most cunning, diabolical detectives ever.

Before John became detective, he was a police officer assigned to one of the toughest areas of Houston, known for its high crime, prostitution, gang violence, and drug infestation. It was an area that even police officers seldom went because of the gang's intricate communication system and disdain for law enforcement. Members would sit atop apartment complexes on every corner, and stood guard twenty-four hours, seven days a week. When police presence was near, soldiers on the ground prepared for the officers' arrival, setting up booby traps in the event of a foot chase and were even known to fire upon approaching police officers.

A few years before John was assigned to the beat, a rookie officer who worked the very area that John was responsible for, spotted some teenage boys walking near an apartment complex in his beat. One of the boys threw a baggie with a white substance into the gutter, and the boys split up, and ran in different directions. The overzealous rookie, threw the police cruiser into park, and despite hearing "Wait!" from his field training officer, he leaped from the driver's seat, and took off on an impressive Olympic sprint to catch one of the perpetrators.

The shadows above his head, perched like massive gargoyles looked down, and proceeded to harmonize whistles that were echoed throughout the complex. The officer continued to run deep into the complex, ignoring his better judgement to retreat and call for back up. He turned a corner, running with all of his might right into a metal fishing wire which had been fashioned, and pulled tight cutting through his neck, and slicing through his trachea. The officer nearly lost his life that day. He was never the same again, and his police career was over.

John was the new rookie to that area, but he saw it as a perfect opportunity to use the activity in this area as a covert playground. An area where police officers had failed the community time and time again, coupled with the racist officers assigned to the beat helped to hide John's indiscretions. He could now regain trust in the community by portraying a philanthropic, community police officer of the people.

During the day, John would ride into the neighborhoods, stop into businesses, and talk to the children; he also got to know the residents, and all the usual suspects, perpetrators, informants, and criminals. It wasn't long before he gained the confidence of the community, who were still careful enough to keep him at arm's length. Their caution was for good reason, for at night he lurked in the shadows, hell-bent on destroying the very ones he had assured that he would protect only hours before.

The nights weren't silent, nor were they holy, as demonic deeds were a mockery to God's promises of peace, joy, and happiness. During the years that John patrolled those streets, the area became known as "Bloody H-Town," for blood spilled into the streets, drained from men, women, and children found lying dead in alleys, trash cans, and fields. Their organs were missing, and the word monster was carved on different areas of the bodies. The workings of a serial killer were at play.

This area housed people who would not be missed; as prostitutes, homeless people, and miscreants only emerged during the cooler temperatures at dusk. Gang members and drug dealers kept the innocent ones imprisoned in their own homes and apartments. People peeked out of their windows; which only blocked the wind on gusty days, but did very little for any other type of protection. Children played outside sometimes, but always looked over their shoulder for the boogeyman that took on many forms. This was the existence for the residents; in an area where the pains of crime did not discriminate or distinguish the good ones from the bad ones.

John interrogated people, made arrests, and exposed gang members suspected of having ties to the crimes, that constantly plagued the area. However, no one was ever directly linked to the mass killings of "Bloody H-Town." These were innocent victims the media portrayed as deserving of their gruesome deaths because of their economic status, neighborhood, or behaviors.

When the killings eventually slowed down, and the arrests of high profile criminals ensued, John was hailed a hero by the department for doing an excellent job in cleaning up the streets. John used his street credibility, his contacts, and his knowledge to become an even better detective. However, his reign of terror was not over. Now as a detective, John could easily move about the city, and manipulate situations in his favor. With a mountain of evidence and suspects he was always privy to, he could set up his traps, plant evidence, and stalk his victims. However, at night, it was time to hunt, and this was his favorite time.

Chapter 7

The early morning was chaotic, as John arrived back at home to reclaim his position at his kitchen table. He took comfort staring out the window that gave him a perfect view of people who never realized that they were in his sights.

However, the chaos was only in his head, as thousands of voices seem to flood his thoughts, causing a massive headache that suddenly made John's nose bleed profusely. He didn't bother to clean up, he just sat there, with blood pouring down his nose, pooling into the crease of his lips, and eventually saturating his teeth, as he opened his mouth to lick the blood.

The blood continued to pour down his chin, and drip onto his chest, as he sat motionless. He finally stood up and poured a cup of hot coffee. John began to whistle which brought the voices from thousands to just one, as he hoped to conjure Dark Man into existence.

John peered into his coffee cup. As he looked down, the reflection he saw on the surface revealed a mirror of his soul.

Stirring the coffee was an act of scrying, as he slowly turned the spoon in small circles, distorting the image. Once the coffee settled back to a motionless mirror, John stared into the cup once again, which revealed a reflection of the demon he had become.

The scrying produced demons, who entered the room, and were willing to do whatever John said, if he was a willing conduit for their manifestation. John sat there whistling "Silent Night," as he now stared out the window in a trance; only getting up to refill his coffee, as he swallowed down cup after cup, wiping blood away from his mouth, until it eventually dried in a sticky mess. The evil spirits filled the room, and entered John, giving him power and ability, which gave John a euphoric release like an intense orgasm.

Just as John seemed to be slipping into a state of euphoria, a voice spoke.

"There is an enemy amongst us, working against our powers," spoke the shrill, hissing, voice that singed through John's soul, like aluminum foil chewed forcefully; making him fall out of his chair, and onto the floor.

He was paralyzed, as the demons reminded him that they controlled him, and not the other way around.

"Someone is praying against us, they are reaching the heavens, and must be removed. We will not be stopped, she must be destroyed! Destroy her, or she will ruin us! Destroy her, or we will ruin you. You know who she is, and you know what you must do!"

John blinked, trying to gather his bearings. He felt the cold hard floor underneath him and knew that he had blacked out. He knew that this would be followed by a migraine. He lifted himself off the ground, and stumbled over to his cabinet, by the kitchen sink. He opened a pill bottle and emptied the contents into his mouth, followed by a gulp of cold coffee.

It seemed as if John was in a time warp, and time had lapsed, eliminating the sunlit morning, leaving John standing in the middle of his kitchen floor, staring out of his window at darkness illuminated by the street light that flickered; as moths covered it for the bit of light that it provided.

"What time is it?" he thought, as he put his fingers across his forehead, and his thumb on his temple, massaging it gently in confusion.

He stood motionless, suddenly thinking about Officer Joyce Anderson, a fellow police officer at the department, as he stared out of his window at the street light that strobed unsystematically. His body began to seize, his vision began to flicker as well, until it dimmed; and once again, there was complete darkness.

***

The all-seeing night was accustomed to witnessing the most horrific activities imaginable; which included murder, and heinous acts of mayhem. Emergency medical services were continuously dispatched; police sirens blaring upon approach, and then fading as they moved quickly to their destinations. Shots rang out, screams filled the air, and fights and brawls were typical. However, on this night, things were different. The screams were of sheer terror and fear, people were running en masse, and there was a panic that could be mutually felt.

There were not enough ambulances to cover the demand, and police S.W.A.T. teams moved throughout the panic-stricken crowds; rushing to scenes of chaos, though it was difficult to ascertain the source. No one stopped long enough to figure out the source; they simply ran, feeling as though something was right on their heels. The police began setting up barriers to isolate the mob into a centralized location in the middle of the city. People ran until they could run no more, right into the barricaded area that swelled with frantic citizens, as everyone tried to figure out why the chaos began.

"Quiet everyone, be quiet!"

It was almost a futile attempt to regain order and quell the crowd; but after several attempts and countless minutes, the crowd fell to a hush. The police commissioner stepped up on a makeshift platform, and spoke loudly into a squealing megaphone.

"There have been some activities that would suggest that safety and security has been compromised in this city; however, we do have a handle on it, and it is within our control. For your continued safety, we must ensure that everyone is cleared to return to your homes and back to your normal lives as quickly as possible. To carry this process out efficiently we must evacuate everyone from this area. You all will be loaded up on buses and will be transported to a more secure location.

Once you have been checked, you will be returned to your homes."

The crowd became suspicious and voiced their skepticism,

"What is this all about?" someone yelled.

"Yeah, what are you not telling us?" "Why should we trust you?" others began to yell.

Shouts of protest filled the air, making it impossible for anyone to think clearly. The riot teams began to utilize a pit formation, to corral the massive crowd towards prepared buses. It was so loud that no one saw or heard the gasps from the group of people that turned around to see that the isolated crowd, were sitting ducks for what was quickly approaching them.

"Oh my God, what is that?" someone exclaimed.

The police commissioner spotted the approaching doom as well.

"Oh my God, we're too late, run!" he yelled to his entourage of top officials that accompanied him to this chaotic scene.

They all jumped into the bullet proof cruisers, and police cars, cranked up, and sped off; mowing down innocent victims in their desperate attempt to leave. As they moved quickly away from the crowd, a few blocks away, they stopped and looked in awe as the streets were filled with torn bodies scattered throughout. There were many horrific scenes of death, and not a single living soul in sight.

The commissioner shook his head, "We were warned, but it happened quicker than we thought," he proclaimed to his companions in the SUV.

"Sir, where do we go?" the driver asked nervously.

"We head to the underground bunker, it is a secret location, and only the elite can go there if something like this ever happens. Driver, stop the car, I'm driving," the commissioner yelled out. He realized that he had strict orders not to disclose the location to anyone except the elite.

"Excuse me, sir?" The driver looked into the rearview mirror, confused.

"Stop the car here, right now!" the commissioner demanded.

The driver complied, and slowed the car down, stopping in a quiet, rich neighborhood that was only divided from the poor neighborhood by an invisible line perpetuated by the strong arms of the law.

"Ok, get out of the car," the commissioner yelled.

The driver stepped out, met by the commissioner, who had already confronted him at the driver's side door. The commissioner slid into the driver's seat, replacing him quickly, as he slammed the door shut, and let the window down.

Smiling maniacally, he said, "Sorry son, you just can't go."

Suddenly, from behind a very beautifully sculptured evergreen bush, stepped a man; his face was distorted, and his mouth was gaped open with blood, that seemed to continuously pour from it. He grabbed the unsuspecting driver from behind, by the shoulders, as the poor driver stood there, still looking into the eyes of the commissioner. This disfigured person pulled him to the ground, as he bit into the side of his neck, and began ravenously eating his body.

The whole scene was so horrific that the commissioner did not notice that the car was now surrounded by what appeared to be people in a different form. Their eyes were completely black, with no life in them, they appeared crazed and wild.

They were also extremely strong, as they began ripping the SUV, which held the elite occupants to shreds, leaving them all vulnerable. Like a can of sardines, the top of the SUV was peeled back, and the occupants were eaten. The commissioner was saved for last, as he was dragged from the driver's seat onto the hot pavement. Five of the dead-like people began biting him and tearing whatever flesh that they could get to. The commissioner made a gurgled, breathless outcry, as blood squeezed into his throat; a cry that went unheard.

"It's too late, the zombie virus is here!"

The orange hue from behind closed lids indicated a sunny day, which John verified when he opened his eyes. John blinked rapidly trying to comprehend how he had ended up outside on the ground, staring up at clouds that shapeshifted every few seconds.

"John, John, open your eyes. Are you ok?" a reassuring voice slowly became clearer and more distinct. "Dear God, in the name of Jesus, I come to you now, asking you to heal my friend John."

"What the Hell do you think you are doing?" John asked the indistinct face attached to the voice ringing in his ears.

He felt blood well up in his throat and turned his head to one side to spit out the metallic tasting red mass; as he looked around deliriously, checking himself over to make sure that he was still intact. He recognized the familiar face staring back at him as that of his fellow co-worker, Officer Joyce Anderson.

"Our Father which are in Heaven hallowed be thy name, thy Kingdom come, thy will be done, on Earth as it is In Heaven," she continued to pray over her wounded friend.

"Stop praying for me, what the hell is wrong with you?" he shouted at her.

"John you're hurt, your head is bleeding, and you are coughing up blood," Joyce said, as she gently placed his shoulders back on the ground. "It's going to be ok, I have an ambulance en route."

Just then, an ambulance approached the scene, and two EMT's jumped out, and began assessing John, who was clearly upset at the help and attention that he was receiving. He was placed on the gurney as he stared into Joyce's eyes, hating her for the kindness that she was trying to bestow.

"What are you doing here? How did you find me?" John asked, as he touched parts of his body again to see if he was intact, realizing he must have been dreaming moments before.

"You dialed my number at 2:00 this morning John, but you did not leave a message. I thought I had better come over and check on you, after no one at the department seemed to know where you were. I'm so glad that I did; they will take care of you John. Don't worry I will be right with you. I will grab your wallet in the house, and lock up and secure everything, and then I will accompany you at the hospital."

John looked in shock and dread, as he thought about his house of horrors, and what she may see if she entered.

"Let me off this thing," he struggled to release himself from the confines of the straps that held him on the gurney.

He tried to speak, but the words were not coming out of his mouth the way that they sounded in his head.

"Now, now, Detective Bigsby, we are going to take very good care of you. Everything is going to be fine," said the EMT as he started an I.V.

The door slammed, and John lay there on the gurney, his blood rapidly coursing through his veins, as the fear of being exposed made him panic-stricken. However, the stress overtook his body as he slowly closed his eyes. He lost consciousness and could no longer formulate a clear thought.

Suddenly, with a huge gasp of air that he seemed to fight to obtain, John raised his body off the floor. He looked around riotously, expecting to find a medical staff running back and forth attending to his needs; but instead, he saw his disarranged kitchen, from a slightly supine position.

He realized that it had all been a dream. He lay there, tasting a glob of blood that he concluded was not a part of the dream. His fingers explored a huge gash in the back of his head as he brought his fingers before his eyes to see the fresh crimson that stained them. He didn't attempt to move. Feeling lethargic and listless, he closed his eyes again.

Chapter 8

The power of prayer was always a formidable force that John was unable to suppress, simply by whistling his comforting tune, which staved off good. Officer Joyce Anderson was a police officer at the same department that John worked for. She even prayed for him when his father died; and when she did, John got a sick feeling in his stomach, and he knew that Officer Anderson was a force that he could not reckon with. His spirit seemed to war with her spirit, which was kind, meek, and humble. Plus, she was very smart, and inquisitive, a trait that threatened John's ability to remain elusive.

She was an officer that worked alongside John's father, Kyle. They went to the police academy together, and because her last name was Anderson, they were alphabetically assigned to partner together. She was responsible for Kyle going to church and turning his life around. They lost touch when Kyle made detective, but every now and then, she would call and encourage Kyle. She knew the struggles that Kyle went through as a police officer in a rough beat, and to take on a son with a tragic upbringing required love, patience, and God. She recognized early on that John was different, and this made her focus her prayers intently on this family. She called upon God, pleading for the blood of Jesus in their lives.

When Kyle passed away she took it very hard and felt responsible for doing whatever she could to help John. She was quickly met with opposition, as John didn't display the appreciation and acceptance the way Kyle had embraced it. Further opposition was felt when other police officers whisked him away into their corrupt lifestyle, keeping her at arm's length.

She stayed away from John, but would whisper a prayer for him anyway, quietly from her desk. John, on the other hand, seethed with anger when he saw her, but could not seem to do anything about it. He wanted her gone; he felt that she was the one person who could see right through him, as if she knew what he was, and this made him very uncomfortable.

She was with the police force for quite a while but was recently assigned to desk duty. She was set to sit before the board to make detective right before being assigned desk duty, a major setback to her demanding work that didn't seem valued.

Coffee brewed, emitting the robust smells of roasted beans heated to perfection. The smell wafted throughout the house, waking Joyce. She stretched, smiling as she realized that her wonderful husband had beaten her to the kitchen to prepare breakfast. She lay in bed for a moment, staring up at the popcorn textured finish, blown onto the ceiling.

It was during these quiet times that she knew that she was very lucky to be alive, each morning; for the streets of Houston were often dangerous and unforgiving for a woman, no matter how adept she was. Lying in bed another second wouldn't shorten the long day that she had ahead, so she threw off the down comforter that enveloped her body, and rose to her feet, as she looked up again beyond the ceiling to say,

"Thank you for another day God."

Joyce could hear the opening and closing of drawers, and the clinking sounds of silverware, as her husband rushed to have everything ready and perfect when his wife joined him downstairs, before rushing off to work.

She smiled again, as she made her way to the bathroom to shower. She hoped the warm water would stave off worry and fear and help reassure her it was going to be a wonderful day. Feeling the warm spray of water hit her skin, and cascade down her body made her feel good, as she lowered her head to make sure that the water hit her neck to ease the tension.

How she wished that she could stand there for hours, and return to the soft bed that seemed to call for her, rejoining the bliss and serenity it offered only moments before. However, she knew that she couldn't, so she cut the shower short, before she could change her mind. Any longer would ensure that she might call in sick, to return to her desired state of repose. She dried off, got dressed quickly, and descended the stairs to enjoy what little time that she could share with her husband, Evan. Evan stood up from the barstool that he was sitting on to greet his wife with a kiss.

"You're going to be late again, sleepy-head," he said.

"I don't care," she said, "Work will be there when I get there. I'm in no hurry."

Tardiness was a not a typical trait of Joyce; she was always an hour early for everything. Lately she seemed burned out, and tired. Evan noticed, and he worried about her. Because he was an R.N. at the biggest trauma center in the city, he knew the signs of stress and fatigue; consequently, as a husband, he knew the signs of burnout and depression as well.

"Hey babe, I think if you took some supplements like L-Carnitine, you would see an increase in your energy levels," he said, as he tried to sound encouraging, and not annoying.

"Stop diagnosing me," she said, as she picked up toast that had obviously been scraped of its burned surface.

She shook her head, and bit into it, chasing it down with a sip of smooth coffee made just the way she liked it.

This morning's agenda included a mandatory meeting which was sure to add more work to the life of a busy police force. The life of a police officer was ever-changing; no two nights or days were ever the same. This used to be an aspect of the job that Joyce liked as a young rookie; but after doing it for several years, it was a trait she came to despise. The unknown kept her stressed, because one moment the night could go smoothly, and in an instant, everything could change, putting her life in jeopardy. After being shot recently, she questioned her decision of joining the force, and she wondered if being a police officer was her calling. Joyce recalled that fateful night like it was yesterday.

It was a late night in February; she was assigned to the graveyard shift at that time. The weather was cold and rainy. Joyce liked it when it was like this, because the streets were fairly quiet. She guessed no one wanted to commit crime in the cold. It was around 3:50 a.m., and she had just checked in from her lunch break. The dispatchers were issuing out response calls to different units, who responded if they were close to the vicinity of the problem.

Nothing major was going on, and Joyce had not received anything at that time, so she decided to patrol a park known for drug trafficking, due to its remote and isolated location. In the daytime, the park was well-known for its walking trails and beautiful botanical scenery. There were lots of trees, and wooded areas that covered more walking trails; and a peaceful brook that trickled serenely that gave this area the perfect back drop for a romance novel. However, at night, this park became the perfect back drop for a horror movie.

This night was no exception, as Joyce spotted a vehicle that looked as if it had ran off of the parking lot, and into a thick copse of trees. The car was only visible by its dash lights, and the engine was still running. Joyce got on her radio and called her location in to dispatch; giving them a description of the vehicle, the time, and her intent to approach the scene.

Just as she stepped out of her car, the rain seemed to come down tumultuously, impairing her vision. She reached back into her car, grabbing her raincoat and flashlight before proceeding to the parked car. Joyce pulled the hood over her head, and ran to the vehicle hurriedly, afraid that someone may be in trouble. She could tell that someone was in the back seat, but the rain made it hard to tell exactly how many people were in the vehicle, and what was going on. She shone the light in the back seat, and saw a man with a small boy. The man did not seem to notice the light, as he was relentlessly raping the listless boy. As she quickly scanned the front seat, she saw another boy, naked and unconscious.

"Hey," she yelled out as she struck the window, causing it to crack instantly due to the frigid conditions outside.

The shattered glass startled the man, and just as Officer Anderson called in for back up, he spun around into a sitting position with a gun, and began firing rounds into her chest. Three struck her bullet-proof vest, and one pierced her shoulder. It blew her to the ground, and she lay there unconscious as the car backed up out of the trees, and sped off, into the night. Rain pelted her body, and she sunk into the mud; bruised, battered, and bloody, until back-up arrived moments later rushing her to the trauma center.

She remembered opening her eyes, alarmed at the sight of faces covered by surgical masks; with looks of concern, yet urgency staring back at her. Her unconscious state eliminated any pain that she may have felt; however, now her mind reminded her that pain should ensue after a traumatic event; and so it did, tremendously. She could not move, and she was sure that the bullets penetrated her chest; the hot slugs spinning through her skin, only stopping after tearing through major organs.

However, this was not the case; the bullet-proof vest did its job, but the impact made it feel otherwise. Her only injury was the bullet that went through her shoulder in the front, and exited through the back, but not before it shattered her scapula. She had surgery, where plates and screws held her together to allow for healing. She wore an arm sling, experienced months of painful physical therapy; and the even more painful experience of desk duty. The worst part of the incident, was the fate of the two boys found in the car. The car was found hundreds of miles away in a small town; inside was the bullet-riddled bodies of the two boys. The monster who did it got away. Although a full investigation was done, no traces of the culprit were found, and it remained an open case. Officer Anderson prayed that it would not turn into a cold case.

Being on desk duty was harrowing. At first, everyone at the department showed concern, and camaraderie; checking on her, helping her around the office, and accommodating her. However, very soon after the incident, internal affairs questioned her about her actions that night. They practically interrogated her, and all but accused her of causing the death of those boys. She already felt guilty and wore the guilt like a wet blanket, rendering her unable to function. It wasn't long before her co-workers and superiors started treating her differently. They threw files on her desk and walked away without speaking. They always seemed to have an inside joke going when she walked into a break room or gathering; because they would giggle as they admonished each other to keep quiet when she walked in. She grew depressed and began to despise work. Her feelings deepened into abhorrence, as she noticed things within the department that she never realized when she worked on the streets.

During that time, she received cases of people being arrested who exhibited strange behaviors. It started with the man who was found in a convenience store. He was completely naked, and his body was cut up from head to toe. Instead of opening the door, and walking into the store, he used his body to go through the door. He banged the window with his head at first, causing a crack, and then he crashed his body into the door again and again, until the door burst into millions of shards slicing through his skin, with some of the bigger pieces of glass lodging into his skin, feet, hands, and face. This did not seem to faze or deter the man, as his blood-filled eyes canvassed the store for a victim.

He looked around wild-eyed, growling, and salivating like a wild dog. The store owner instantly called the police, as people who stood in line, tried to scramble to get out of the way. The naked man grabbed an unfortunate man who wasn't quick enough and took him to the ground. He began to practically eat the man alive; biting his face and neck, stopping to chew and swallow the flesh.

The poor victim lay there kicking and writhing in pain, as he let out blood-curdling screams every time this animalistic man took a bite out of him. The police arrived, and ordered the naked man to stop; however, the man looked up for a second, growling viciously like a bear, as he peeled back his lips, revealing teeth that he used as a warning not to approach. A police officer pulled out his taser, sending two prongs into the torso to deliver an eight second burst, but this only enhanced the anger and violence, as the naked man moved toward the police officers. It was as though he felt no pain. The cops fired shots into the man who continued to try to attack. However, his rage was no match for bullets, as he fell to the ground letting out a final eerie growl; as he expired on the bloody, and glass-filled floor.

News crews converged upon the scene immediately, as police choppers, and news helicopters circled and swarmed above. A huge crowd gathered, making the scene chaotic, as word spread very quickly about the incident.

Police tape kept the crowd at bay, as investigators, detectives, police officers, and forensic teams lifted the tape to walk in and out of the confined area. The victim survived and was rushed to the hospital. The scene was processed for hours, with the naked bloody man slowly going into rigor mortis until the medical examiner came, and finally took him away for an extensive autopsy. The scene left a lasting impression on everyone there, as kids, neighbors, friends, and bystanders looked at the uncovered shredded body of the naked man.

Autopsy revealed a combination of drugs in the man's system, and this was released to the public immediately. The media's report of drugs helped to justify a good reason for feelings of contentment at his death by cop. So, after the report was broadcast on the news, people shook their heads in disgust and confirmation as they thought, felt, and said,

"Just another drugged-up crack head, that's what you expect from those people," and life moved on.

However, as a good police officer, and the wife of a great nurse, she felt that this was more than just a cocktail of street drugs. The strangest part of the case was the announcement that was made right after the autopsy was revealed. They were able to link this man to the murders of all the victims found in "Bloody H-Town."

Joyce knew that this was impossible. The time line just did not add up, and Joyce personally knew this man, and he was not the crazed person that was portrayed. Plus, it would have been physically impossible for the man to commit such crimes, given his physical and mental limitations.

There seemed to be a cover-up, as the case was handed over to higher authorities, and quickly closed. Portions of the file were handed to Joyce to close out. She was instructed to treat the case like an expungement, erasing all evidence that it ever existed. Men walked into the police department in dark suits, spoke with the police chief, and walked out with files tucked away protectively in their briefcases. Joyce found this to be quite strange, as totally erasing everything about such a high-profile case, or any case, was not customary. Joyce wondered how this would be handled in court as the families, and the public, sought answers.

This case was just one of many strange occurrences that happened in the city. Nothing was strange to a police department that had heard it all. However, just when they thought that they had heard it all, something weirder would take place. Still, it was never strange enough to be impossible. It was hard to determine if an epidemic of illness, madness, or drugs, was plaguing the streets.

There were also the constant cases of missing persons, which kept the telephones at the station ringing. There were unsolved murders every day. The police station was never quiet; it was always in a state of highly charged pressure and tension. Police officers worked very hard, only to be berated for the actions of the corrupt ones that were showcased on the news.

Joyce didn't know what the meeting this morning would entail, but she was sure that it was something that would take precedence over everything else that had gone awry in the city. She donned her uniform reluctantly, as she thanked her husband for a wonderful start to an uncertain day, by kissing him softly on his lips.

"Gotta go," she said, as he grabbed her tiny wrist gently to pull her back in for reassurance of his love.

"I know, I do too," he said. "It's going to be alright, you know," he reassured her with a smile."

The police station was chaotic as always, officers running in and out, suspects cursing and talking loudly, phones ringing off the hook, and people filing paperwork, or waiting at the desk to speak with a watch commander, or detective.

"Anderson!" one of the supervisors called out, as she walked into her department. "I need you to follow up on some evidence that you submitted from the murders on Riverdale Drive. Get on the phone and call the lab, follow up with the forensics team, the coroner's office, and get that information to me ASAP. Oh, and call Biggs at home, and let him know what is going on, and also let him know that internal affairs wants to schedule a meeting with him tomorrow."

"But sir, don't they have a secretary to do that in the detective division? I have been calling Detective Bigsby for days with no answer sir. Plus, I am supposed to see the chief about being released back to street duty, right after the meeting," she said. "Sir, I really need to talk to you about...."

He ignored her, as he continued to walk around the corner out of earshot.

Joyce stood in the middle of the floor silently, as chaos ensued around her. She slowly turned and walked to a cubicle to begin her phone calls. She was tired of the treatment she was receiving, the extra work that they piled on her, and the place of darkness that they always kept her in.

They gave her evidence to process from the double homicide of the couple brutally murdered in their home. It was John's case, but for some reason they gave her the daunting task of sending evidence to the lab, checking phone records of the victims, and making important phone calls. This was clearly the work for the other detectives, and she knew they were just dumping work on her as usual.

She tried once to speak to the chief concerning everything that was bothering her about the department, and her ill-treatment, but the chief gave her the impression that if she couldn't handle her job, maybe she should reconsider her career.

"Everyone is experiencing a tremendous amount of work, Anderson," he said with condescending overtones. "I got the media, internal affairs, and everyone else looking over our shoulders. I got officers denied days off, due to shortage. We got things going on, and everyone is feeling the pull and you're complaining about some work piled up on your desk.

Can you handle this job, Anderson? I need your head in the game, and lately it seems that you haven't been in the game. This puts the whole department at a disadvantage, when you are not focused. Either be part of the solution or be part of the problem away from this department."

Joyce knew from that day on that she was totally on her own, which was a sad, lonely, and scary place to be. She had been secretly seeing a therapist to help deal with depression and anxiety. She felt that she was on the verge of a nervous breakdown an admission that she had made to her therapist weeks before. She considered calling in sick this morning, but "mandatory" meant that there was no excuse except death.

Joyce sat at her cubicle and looked at the clock on her desk, realizing the meeting was starting in 15 minutes. She decided that informing Detective Bigsby about the meeting this morning was futile. She decided to leave a message on voicemail about the internal affairs meeting. She dialed the number and listened as the phone continued to ring repeatedly. Just as she was about to leave a message, she heard a voice on the other end.

"Detective Bigsby?" she said. "Sir, this is Officer Joyce Anderson with the Houston Police Department. I have been instructed to call you about a meeting with Mr. Doug Sessions tomorrow morning at 7 a.m."

Just then, an internal affairs agent walked up to her desk, as he waited for her to finish talking. When she finished informing John about his meeting, she slowly lowered the phone back onto the receiver.

"Officer Anderson, come with me please."

Chapter 9

John was awakened by the series of rings from his cell phone that must have carried on for some time, because he thought that he was experiencing ringing in his head constantly. He slowly rose from the cold, hard, unforgiving floor, which he assumed was his bed for days, as he noticed that his clothes smelled of urine. There was also a dried outline of pooled urine beneath him, and a vast area of dried blood where his head rested.

Blurry vision began to slowly clear up, as he squinted at the screen of his phone that he retrieved from the floor next to him. He quickly realized that he had missed dozens of calls. His thumb glided over the answer icon, as the phone began to ring again displaying the, "unknown caller" contact. A voice emitted, that haunted him more than the weird state in which he found himself.

"Detective Bigsby?" "Sir, this is Officer Joyce Anderson with the Houston Police Department. I have been instructed to call you about a meeting with Mr. Doug Sessions tomorrow morning at 7 a.m."

"What day is it?" John asked.

"Sir, are you ok?" she asked with sincere concern.

He didn't wait for an answer, and didn't bother to respond as his thumb slid over the feature that would eliminate any further conversation.

He stumbled to his feet, using the counter for support, as his legs continued to wobble, and steer him back and forth, awaiting the brain to assist them with stabilization. A glass sitting on the counter nose-dived onto the floor below, shattering into a thousand pieces, as John attempted to reach for it. When that failed, he simply turned the coffee pot up to his lips, drinking the remaining cold coffee that sat collecting spores, and bacteria from the nasty conditions of the house.

He stumbled to the bathroom, as he removed his clothing, making a trail with every garment that he left behind on his way there. He turned on the water, and stepped inside the shower, before the water could even turn warm.

The cold liquid electrified him, waking him up from his clouded state. Red water pooled underneath his feet, reminding him of the deep laceration that now throbbed, as the water cleaned the wound, and exposed the nerves that were protected from dried caked up blood, and scabbed tissue.

After a quick shower, he stepped out of the tub, still feeling a little groggy, but better than before. He went to the bedroom and sat down on his bed, picking up the phone to address some of the missed calls.

Listening to some of the missed messages, he heard one that he received a couple of days before, from one of the detectives. It was his partner that vowed allegiance to his friend John.

"Hey buddy, we processed that murder over on Riverdale Drive. No worries, I headed up the case, we don't have any good leads yet, but I did get back the results of some fingerprints that I want to talk to you about. Call me as soon as you get this message so that we can meet up and talk. Thanks, bye."

John knew who it was; he was a veteran detective that took John under his wing after John's father died. Chris was a good detective, he was a lot like John, in that he stayed to himself, took care of business, and always covered for his fellow detectives when necessary. John lowered the phone from his ear, and stared at the lit screen until it dimmed, and went black, awaiting further operation. Contemplating his next move, his right knee began to bounce, indicating nervousness that he had not experienced in a long time.

His abuse made him stronger, more confident in himself, or so he thought. He had endured extreme conditions that would make or break a person. However, he didn't realize that he was indeed broken, and not as strong as he thought he was; in fact, he had cracked. During extreme abuse, in which a dominant figure intended to brainwash, manipulate, and control a person, the conditions are so horrific and extreme, that the person cracks, and disassociates, unable to control their own thought processes. They became the perfect candidate for mind control.

John was controlled; implanted deep in his inner self was Dark Man, who constantly reminded him that failure was not an option. He must carry out an assignment directed by Dark Man; otherwise, he feared the extreme headaches would one day make his head explode. John was driven, not only by the fear of pain, torture, or death, but the need to succeed. He thought that he was in control of his insatiable desire to successfully kill; he was terribly deceived, as the demonic forces that encompassed him, laughed and mocked him, torturing his mind.

A demon emerged from within him, and immediately sat him straight up, stopped his knee from bouncing, and puckered his lips, forcing air through them, as he pushed out the shrill whistled version of, "Silent Night," in a twisted rendition. He continued whistling as his thumb glided over the screen of his phone again, and he dialed the number to call back his fellow detective.

"Biggs," the detective answered instantly, "Where the Hell have you been?"

"Hey Chris, I had some personal business that was important. What's up?"

"I don't trust these phones. How about we meet somewhere."

"What's up with internal affairs?" John asked, upset about the inconvenience of being called in.

"No worries, Biggs, don't worry about it; it has been taken care of. Let's meet at our usual spot in two hours."

John hung up, his breathing immediately erratic, and his carotid artery became visible as it pulsated with boiling blood. He stood up from the bed and picked up his boots, tossing them at the door so that he could step into them on his way out. He began to whistle as he got dressed, looking out the window, at the dawn of morning which had not yet lit the sky. John slipped away from the house, another maniac trolling the streets and highways of Houston.

***

John drove down a long road, his car rocked from side to side, as the tires worked to climb over huge rocks and debris. He could see the dark colored SUV in the distance as he approached. As he closed the distance between himself and the SUV, he could see the detective standing in front of his parked vehicle, a cigarette tucked tightly between his lips, and two coffee cups sitting on the hood.

"You look like shit," Chris said, extending his hand to John, as John exited his car and walked towards him.

"Good morning to you too, sunshine," John said, tightly gripping his hand, and then moving past him to the coffee.

John took a couple of gulps of coffee and turned around to lean his body on the front panel of the SUV as he carefully crossed his feet.

"So, no leads yet on our case huh?" John said almost with a chuckle.

"John, you are a part of an elite group of detectives, which is quite an honor considering the perks that it brings. One of those perks is allegiance and protection. When your father died, we all swore to protect and serve you, and we will always do that, but it comes with a price. Your dad Kyle, paid the price, he was a good man.

You work for the police department, and your job is to help find and clean the scum off the streets so that my kids, and your future kids and family, can be safe and enjoy the world that our forefathers built. We know what we are here to do; the public has a different perspective about what we do because of sloppy, amateur, police officers and detectives. Making the news because of a shooting on an innocent civilian is sloppy. We don't need that kind of attention. We are elite, we are not sloppy," Chris said, stepping up to John's face, as his eyes narrowed.

John uncrossed his legs and raised his body off of the vehicle to take a defensive stance, as he balled up his fist.

Chris laughed, "Stand down, you don't want to make that mistake pal. Keep your nose clean, solve crimes, and do what you are told, and you will go very far. Screw that up, expose the brotherhood of blue, and you die, it's as simple as that."

Suddenly, John felt seven years old again as he stared down at the dirt, fists still clenched, and now his jaw tightened and clenched as he trembled with anger.

"Internal affairs will talk with you tomorrow, it's going to be fine; they want to talk to you about the case. Don't worry about saying much, we have already taken care of everything for you. Just show up, and shut up."

Chris then reached into his pants pocket, pulling out a piece of paper.

"Take care of this, Biggs," Chris held the paper in front of John's downcast eyes, and he slowly brought the paper up, causing John to make eye contact with him. "We have work to do, let's get it done," he said, playfully punching John on the shoulder.

"Let's keep the streets quiet tonight, make it a silent night," Chris said, as John went into a near-catatonic state.

Chris brushed past him and climbed into his SUV. He drove away and left John standing in the field, gripped by a phrase that would determine his course of action for the night, which would inevitably creep upon the Earth, and unfortunately darken someone's life.

Chapter 10

An empty body and an empty soul is what the daybreak found, when the sun had just peeked above the Earth. In the cold dirt lay a boy, with his organs missing; including the eyes, which were often seen as windows to the soul. Eyes that would never again be forced to see the evil that this world had to offer; and he would not have to succumb to its reign ever again.

Just as habeas corpus was an order intended to bring the body before the court, the whistled tune that preceded this massacre was an order to bring the insides of the body before the evil judge. That is precisely what happened, as the organs were excised from the innocent child to be used for vile intentions. Silence and stillness would not be interrupted here, for no one would ever know that this final resting place was where the body would return to dust, the bones bleached by the sun, and the memory mourned by the broken-hearted loved ones forever.

Sweat popped up and began to cascade down a forehead wrinkled with signs of distress. It was quickly absorbed by an oily rag, so as not to trickle down, stinging the eyes and distorting the grisly view. This place was one of many makeshift graveyards used to hide a body, a horrible injustice to grieving families.

Years ago, this area became the undiscovered burial ground for many missing persons. However, in recent years bodies were discovered in its killing fields; the workings of a serial killer they thought, perhaps the I-45 Killer as the police dubbed him. Perhaps, there was more than one killer, as the body count rose. They never found the killer, or killers, who buried bodies who did not deserve to be separated from their loved ones in this manner.

There was more than one killer for this area. John knew this, because he was one of them. Some of the bodies were his doing, but many of them were not. This was perfect, because his job as a detective gave him the right to be in wrong places. He could link discovered bodies to other bodies, keeping his identity as a willing participant well hidden, while disguising himself as the hero for bringing cold cases one step closer to being solved. John had many areas he was privy to, areas in which he could dispose bodies.

Refineries were off limits to the public; they were remote, oftentimes, swampy, desolate, and populated with snakes, crocodiles, rats, and other wildlife. There were heavily wooded areas with thick trees, and brush that made a wall, hiding the marshy ground behind its protective front. These areas were breeding grounds for mosquitoes and poisonous frogs; it was vast with poison ivy, stickers, and dangerous animals.

There were places that became accustomed to violent crime, where people guarded themselves as best that they could, but still had to carry on with life, in hopes that it would not be their last time. There were also the not-so-obvious places, which consisted of huge mansions, warehouses, beautiful suburban homes and businesses, and desolate country homes in the middle of nowhere, daycare facilities, churches, hospitals, and office buildings where evil took place.

John didn't have to work hard to find a place to hide his indiscretions; the city hid it for him; just like it hid the indiscretions of the many serial killers who stalked and preyed on the Houston streets. These bodies were the victims that found a resting place that would eventually return their bodies to the dust.

However, there were missing people who would never be laid to rest in this manner, their bodies would never be found by forensic investigation. Trafficking, rituals, and sacrifices resulted in the most hideous disposals of the human body. John could get away with murder, and simultaneously promise closure to families, although he knew justice would truly never be served.

The killer walked away from the scene; human entrails and organs carefully placed in the back of his red F-150. He climbed in, wiping his brow again; smudging more oil on his face than removing the sweat that poured down. Tossing the rag on the floor board, he cranked the engine and slowly drove

104 • *Cortina Jackson*

away. Smoke from the refineries in the distance decorated his rearview mirror. A few miles, and some turns, helped him to blend into the morning commute on I-45. He quickly became just another citizen.

***

A look of worry and confusion from Officer Joyce Anderson was dismissed by the unflinching scowls of the three men who sat in silence across the table from her. The men scribbled notes onto pads, and looked up occasionally at the officer. Files were strewn across a long table in the conference room that held silence in, and freedom out.

"Officer Anderson, you have been with the department for a long time, haven't you?" One of the men finally asked.

"Yes, I have," her voiced cracked, as she used the nervousness in her stomach to push out her voice.

"How do you like it?" he continued, "The job, I mean."

"I have always wanted to be a police officer," she spoke, "ever since I was a little girl."

"You didn't answer my question," he said, as the other two men looked on, eyes narrow and accusatory.

"Officer Anderson, you were shot about a year or so ago during an incident that you conducted. The two boys from that case were murdered. How did all of that make you feel?"

"How did it make me feel? I felt horrible!" she said swallowing back tears. "It was the most devastating thing that I have ever been through."

Welled-up tears finally fell down her cheeks. She quickly wiped them away with her hand, but it was futile; they poured down uncontrollably.

"It's been pretty tough on you, hasn't it?" another one of the men chimed in.

"Yes, it has," she said, "But I think that I am ready to go back out on the streets. The doctor has given me a full release, and I think being back out there will help me mentally and emotionally."

The men looked at each other and began to shuffle through their notes.

"You have had a pretty tough time mentally, haven't you? Do you know what PTSD is, Officer Anderson?"

"Well yes, I know that it is post-traumatic stress disorder."

"Yes, that's right, it makes it pretty hard to recover after experiencing a terrifying event. Getting shot is terrifying isn't it? Losing two kids in a case that you were involved in…"

"Now wait a minute!" Joyce spoke up, "Are you trying to diagnose me? Are you a doctor?"

"Oh, no ma'am, I'm simply asking questions today, I'm in no way trying to imply that you have PTSD. Although, you have used the employee assistance program, and sought the services of a therapist, is that right?"

"Officer Anderson, the fact of the matter, is that your work has suffered tremendously, even while being on light duty. You have been responsible for evidence that is critical to cases that will be going to court. Innocence and guilt is based upon evidence, it cannot be compromised in any way. How would you feel if the person that murdered those two boys got away, because the evidence was mishandled?"

"I have not mishandled evidence," Joyce said, "I do my job, and I do it well, even when work has been piled up on my desk; work that I was not responsible for, I still took care of it."

"Well now, that is not totally true is it, Officer Anderson? Just recently, Detective John Bigsby's case has been greatly compromised. There were phone calls that were never made, and evidence that was never submitted. This whole case is in jeopardy, and we don't have answers.

This is not the first time, Anderson; we have had very critical evidence, and files that you processed that were not handled properly. After the murder of those two boys, you were found to have been negligent; you didn't wait for back up; you didn't follow proper procedures."

The man slammed his fist on the table.

"But we articulated that case well, so that you wouldn't get sued, and we kept you employed here, giving you a job with light duty, because the Chief spoke so highly of you. However, this misconduct on your part is no longer going to be tolerated; you are a liability. Mrs. Anderson, will you please relinquish your weapon and badge? I'm afraid that you are terminated at this time."

The men stood up, and two of them came around the table to make sure that her weapon was handed over with no problems. The other man called the Chief on his cell phone, so that he could see Officer Anderson off the facility. The Chief entered the conference room almost immediately as Joyce was handing over her weapon to the men. The weight of her duty belt being handed over was a load lifted; not only physically, but mentally, as she felt sad, but free. The Chief looked sad and disappointed.

"Anderson, I will make sure that you have a clear F-5, which will show that you were terminated for reasons other than misconduct. I'm so sorry, and I wish you luck."

The Chief extended his hand; Joyce looked down at it with a smirk, and immediately noticed a symbol on his wrist, as his jacket and watch slid back slightly, revealing its presence.

"You have your work cut out for you, Chief. I pray that you are extended the same courtesy that you have extended to me," she said with a hint of sarcasm. "Good day, gentlemen."

With that, she walked away from the police department with her head held high, and her heart open to receive the positive things absent in her life for many years. She was now ready to protect and serve in other capacities and give back to the community that had long been robbed of real justice. This wasn't an end to a career, it would be the beginning of change. For what was done in the dark, had to come to the light.

Chapter 11

There erupted a great rumbling, and thick bellows of smoke that rose from the very depths of Hell, for Satan grew restless and livid. He knew that his time was near when he would no longer have free reign over the Earth.

Prayers were being dispatched all over the world for God's will to be done on Earth as it was in Heaven. God listened intently, as His name was being called for help from a distressed nation. This was unacceptable to Satan who had worked so hard to keep people distracted and discouraged. It seemed to be backfiring, as people were calling on the name of the Lord to heal the land.

Satan pounded his mighty fist into the liquid fire that splashed into a mighty tsunami. Screams and moans that already roared throughout the overcrowded furnace of despair only elevated to a new high as the molten lava enveloped their souls and rose over the great canyons and mountains of Hell;

spilling into each of the millions of tunnels that held weary souls.

There was such a fury in Hell that even the Earth felt the effects. Fires began to burn in various places on Earth, tornadoes touched down in places not known for tornadic activity, and tropical storms began to brew, ready to unleash their disdain for the disturbance. Satan himself called upon legions of demons ready to carry out assignments that would release them from their torture.

"Why are people calling on Him?" he said with a crescendo that made the lava began to boil, as the stench from liquefied souls of millions of rotted inhabitants rose into his flared nostrils. The demons trembled, trying not to make eye contact, as Satan's glare narrowed into a nightmarish scowl.

"I want answers!! Why are the mortals calling on Him for help? Have we not taken everything from them? Have we not depressed them, hurt them, maimed them, and confused them?"

Maniac's forked tongue darted out, as he answered with a hiss,

"Master Satan, we have turned many against God."

Satan grabbed him quickly by the throat.

"We do not mention His name here!!" he reminded him as he pulled him close into his terrifying face, breathing his poisonous breath into Maniac's menacing stare, which caused his eyes to melt from the sockets.

Maniac fell to the ground writhing in pain blindly, as he savagely began cutting himself with his razor sharp finger nails.

He realized that his mistake, in mentioning God was stupidity. Satan stuck his fingers into the sockets, and lifted Maniac off the ground.

"If you ever make that mistake again, I will have the imps to eat that tongue, and burrow into your throat, eating your insides for eternity!! You oversee these legions that should be bringing more souls to me! You and the other lead devils and demons had better get the job done! You had better go to each person that is praying and make them surrender to me. I want full allegiance.

I have a plan that is to be put in place, the humans that have already pledged to follow me will be used and destroyed. You are to go to the ones who are on the fence about salvation, the young children who are easily influenced, the racists, the wounded, the sick, the poor, the defenseless, and especially the Christians; I want them infiltrated immediately!!"

Satan began to look around his vast underworld at all the demons, devils, imps, and souls that begged for release to join the great satanic army that would enter Earth. As he spoke of his master plan, his thunderous voice echoed and covered the deafening shrieks and crying the weary souls could not contain.

"There is to be a plan that will be different from all of the other plans and abhorrent agendas that are currently being carried out in the world. It is to be a carefully executed plan that will call for the allegiance of many organizations, secret societies and sects, to seek a culling and self-purging of society.

Nothing in the world is happening by chance or accident; we rule the Earth. The poor are poor, and it is to be kept that way; and the rich are to be kept wealthy, healthy, and in power, so they think they rule the world. Stupid mortal humans! I want the rich and elite to be influenced, to feel as if people underneath their status are depleting the resources they feel that they are solely entitled. Some of them will take a stand and form organizations to bring balance back to the world. They worship me, and perform rituals that welcome us to their world; and some of them spread the hate and evil, that in which, we specialize. They are very willing to do whatever I tell them, and in turn, I give them feigned power. Their ignorance delights me, so continue to influence their decisions.

I want children to be influenced, they are the next generation. Hurt them, abuse them, brainwash them so that they will continue to work for me, without even realizing their ignorant blind allegiance.

Go to the satanic orders, the organizations, the sects, the groups, and the secret societies, and plague their thoughts with plans for evil. They will be kept healthy by gleaning and harvesting the bodies of the weak. They eat the flesh of women, men, boys, and girls; for eating the flesh, and drinking the blood of another living being empowers them. They will absorb the energy and life force of the person, making them feel younger, faster, stronger, and more powerful. When their bodies fail them, they are to get replacement parts from the sacrifices they offer up to me, and I will grant them longevity, and ensure them immortality. Hahaha... their immortality will serve them well in Hell!

I want them all to be brainwashed, so they feel that diseases are brought on by the poor who are affecting their pure quality of life. Continue to make them feel that their money, and hard-earned tax dollars are going to people who only accept handouts, and only cripples society. I want the masses to formulate the idea that the undesirables in society, or the ones beneath their status, are pulling on the Earth's natural resources, and in a few years, the Earth's water supply, oil supply, and natural resources will be dried up, due to overpopulation, and global warming.

Use the media to control the minds of people, so that subliminal messages reveal that different races and groups of people are contributing to the crime, pollution, and uprisings; they are adding nothing, but taking everything, thus bankrupting and depleting nations.

Influence the radio stations so that they put out music and messages of a negative connotation; and no more subtle messages in the children's cartoons. I want there to be blatant racism, sexism, and Satanism displayed in the kids programming, so that their weak little minds are captured, and set in stone.

These things will help our cause, as people see that their future generations are in jeopardy. If every one of you do your job right, the world will turn on itself, snuffing out human health, quality of life, and the existence of God, leaving a weak, dying populace. People will be in such a trance that they will go along with it. They will hate each other, they will kill each other, and they will go into complete chaos, creating a self-purge that will make our job very easy.

You must stand ready to take lives instantly; at the very moment that these feeble-minded mortals exhale their last breath, I want you to be there so you can deposit them straight to Hell. For in this state of chaos, no one will call upon a God that has not rescued them from the Hell on Earth. Hahahaha… As below, so above, now take Hell to the Earth, and bring the Earth to Hell!!!"

Demons carefully orchestrated the plans on the Earth. It was true, nothing in the world happened by chance or accident. The poor were poor for a reason, and sometimes the poverty line was drawn so obscurely, that common-folk could not comprehend its boundaries. Only the elite could see that it was a straight line with 99 percent of the people underneath it. Those who couldn't see it, or refused to see it, could not understand the agenda that the line was drawn for in the first place, and therefore it worked.

On the other side of the line was the very wealthy, healthy, and powerful. They could see their line clearly, they were the entitled 1 percent. The deception that the elites wanted to purport was that the top 10 percent of the world was accepted. However, the elites never had any intention of including anyone beneath their status. Once again, only those with open eyes could see the bigger picture.

There were new lines constantly drawn that continued to keep separation amongst people. However, evil and malevolence crossed all the lines; it did not discriminate, it saw the lines, and attempted to take the lines and use them as nooses to choke out every person in the world. This made room for some of the most heinous deeds to be perpetrated, and there were many willing participants to help carry out the deeds. Serial killers, rapist, abusers, oppressors; there were plenty of takers that fulfilled their own pleasures by causing hurt, torture, mayhem, and death.

The evil spirits were restless and wanted to speed up the process of elimination. They had to press upon the elites, that it was time to begin their reign. Hopelessness would help create a faster method of eliminating the undesirables, for if they felt that all hope was gone, they would give up praying, and believing in God; and could be easily killed off in their weakened state.

Eventually, all that would be left in the world would be the elite. With the elite comfortably in place, there would be no more resistance from hopeful, praying people. The demons could easily infiltrate the one percent who vowed allegiance to a satanic power. Killing them would be easy.

The poverty stricken areas were basically already bleeding out and gangs, drugs, and incarceration of the heads of households were doing the handy work of the elite, who desperately wanted to eliminate everyone.

The demons began their work long before, working in stages to prepare for the moment when worldwide domination would be at hand. The first stage was easy to initiate, cripple communities. They infiltrated neighborhoods, and introduced drugs, and guns, so that crime would explode to an all-time high. Lengthy sentences for crimes committed, ensured that the incarcerated ones could not come back to protect their neighborhoods from a much worse adversary.

Major corporations and businesses pulled out of neighborhoods and communities in certain cities, causing jobs to be pulled away as well; crippling the cities, so that the communities could not thrive. Panic, fear, and desperation abounded, as fathers were not be able to provide for their families. The communities became crime-ridden, and poverty-stricken, as people resorted to doing whatever they had to do, just to survive, even if that meant contributing to their own problems.

The next stage was sepsis of the communities, neighborhoods, towns, and cities. Entire communities were poisoned by genetically modified food, tainted water, vaccines, and air pollutants. Subpar medical treatment, and medications that caused other health issues and complications, weakened and killed numerous people, and affordable healthcare was hard to obtain.

The vaccines that were introduced, were laced with many different substances, and people were unaware of what they were really hosting in their bodies. Water systems were tainted with fertilizers, drugs, and poisons. This caused numerous health problems for the residents that had no other choice but to drink, and bathe with it.

The debauchery planned ensured that young mothers became sterile, so that they were unable to bring forth new life. Abortion clinics were readily available, encouraging women who could barely care for themselves, to have an alternative.

The rest of the generations were born with ailments, mental illnesses, sicknesses and diseases.

The next stage included fear, distrust, smokescreens, and racial divides; because together we stand, but divided we fall, and workers of iniquity counted on the big fall. Racial divides grew wider and wider making people realize that there were consequences for crossing the invisible line that divided people.

The demons had to use this to their advantage, because it was a problem that had persisted for centuries, and would work as a great segue to deep seated hatred on any side of the racial line. Marches and protests would soon not be peaceful anymore, as people would realize that there was no justice and no peace. If peace could be killed, then there would be all out riots, war, and mayhem. For the last effort was to eradicate them all, no matter their race, gender, or identity.

Everyone thought that they were above everyone else, when on the whole scheme of things, the desire was to destroy the entire world so that they would reside in Hell, where Satan and his evil doers were destined to be. Failing was not an option. The demons began to unite, as they prepared for worldwide domination. They began to join forces with demons called upon by the many leaders in the world who came together to discuss the politics of the land. Once all the elites were in place, and the powers of evil had been summoned, the plan was revealed. The final stage of the plan was now at hand.

There was a meeting simultaneously taking place on Earth, as a meeting taking place in Hell. Suddenly, Satan spoke with a malodorous bellow that filled the air with a stifling sickness that befell the most hardened demon. Both worlds listened intently as ill intentions filled the atmosphere.

"The time has come for us to take our places in the land, and rule. No longer will our mouths be shut, no longer will our deeds be hidden, for we are the rightful heirs to a world that is being destroyed by undesirables. It is time to introduce the final stage of the annihilation of the poor, weak, sick, and criminal. It is something that has been introduced to people for many years, and they didn't even know that it sat dormant, waiting to be birthed."

Satan laughed, and raised his massive arms above his head, at the exact moment the elite leader on Earth raised his arms, as they both announced,

"Unleash the zombie demons, and do on Earth as it is in Hell."

Chapter 12

Hell on Earth was precisely what the world seemed to have become, as John scrolled down the news app on his computer reading story after story of countless murder sprees across the nation. There were many senseless killings, of what appeared to be normal people simply snapping, to commit some of the most heinous crimes imaginable.

Missing persons cases were becoming top news, as they were occurring by the dozens in cities everywhere. Spree killings and mass murders seem to happen before the world could recover from the initial events.

John drank his coffee; staring at the screen. He opened several windows on the computer so that he could involve himself in the chat rooms, troll social media pages, look at the news stories, and watch graphic pornography that didn't serve to get him off, but rather enrage him to carry out more heinous deeds. A news story broke that caught John's attention. He watched intently as he recognized some of the police detectives that stood by, caught in the view of the camera.

"If you see something, say something. Our children are missing. My son Aiden is missing; another child is now missing. Someone knows what's going on."

Five women stood with pictures of their missing children displayed for everyone to see on the morning news. They each took turns begging into the camera.

"Please, if you have my child, I beg you to return them, no questions asked, please!"

One of the women collapsed in despair.

A task force assembled to check a radius that extended from the vicinity of the missing children's homes, all of whom lived in the same area. Candlelight vigils were held, search groups went out every day, and families held out hope, although tears flowed constantly from the fear that they may never see their loved ones again.

John knew the routine, but he was a homicide detective, not a missing persons detective. His job began once a body was found, and he was sure he would not get that call for a long time to come, for they would never find a body if he could help it.

John reached up to carefully move his fingers across the deep laceration on the back of his head. It throbbed and pulsed like a heartbeat, and blood covered his fingertips as he held his hand before his eyes. He stood up and grabbed a sour towel that lay balled up on the counter top and pressed it on the infected wound, as the blood seeped into the fibers, enough to temporarily stop the bleeding. Despite his dizziness, he grabbed his suit jacket, turned off the computer, and stepped outside to greet the day that consisted of his meeting with internal affairs. As his car slowly moved down the street, he unwrapped a piece of gum and shoved it into his mouth.

He reached up to grab his shades that were tucked behind his visor, just in time to cover the evil stare that he presented to three young girls that playfully giggled at a stop sign. The mirrored reflection only gave the girls the impression that a nice man was glancing their direction, not the reptilian stare that truly reflected evil intentions. They smiled and waved, and continued giggling, as the car behind him honked the horn, indicating that John had sat longer than he realized. He jumped, and snapped out of the trance as he accelerated forward, still glancing in his side mirror at the trio.

The commute to the police department seemed exceptionally long, blurring as miles and miles of traffic seemed to endlessly create a warping effect. Taillights strobed as commuters hit their brakes, horns blew from every inch of the freeway, and sirens could be heard in the distance every few miles. John inched down the highway, but never knew exactly how he got to work.

He seemed to be off lately, and wondered if he did real damage when he hit his head. His dreams were vivid, his desires were insatiable, but his focus was obscured. He sat in his car for just a bit, staring at the door to the back entrance meant for personnel. He looked away, but quickly looked back, noticing the dark menacing figure that always plagued his thoughts. Dark Man suddenly stared in John's direction, hovering like a hideous apparition, he then turned away, and slipped through the closed door.

"You're not real, you're not real!" John realized. He surprised himself, that he finally made such an epiphany.

John grabbed his head, squeezing his eyes shut. "I am losing my mind, I am going crazy, I must..."

John shook his head, trying to rid his mind of a nightmare, and opened his eyes to find Dark Man staring at him face to face. His bulging yellow eyes stared deep into John's, cutting through his pupils, and burning an image of terrifying evil within the retinas, which reflected an undeniable evil, that did exist. John's mouth gaped open, and a terrifying fear enveloped his soul. He gripped the steering wheel for support, as he locked his arms, trying his best to brace himself from falling over.

"Hey John, they're ready for you inside, you better get going," said a detective standing at John's driver's side window, with his knuckle rapping against the glass.

"Yeah, I'm going," John mumbled, still confused and scared; as he looked around the car really quick to see if he was alone. He was.

John exited his vehicle, carefully shutting the door, and continued to look around, as he badged in to the controlled access door, and entered the building. The police department was filled with the same rigmarole. It was this insanity that made John sane, as chaos and confusion was his norm.

He went down a hallway to the conference room for the internal affairs investigation. He noticed a few detectives from his division were standing around. As one of the detectives was coming out of the meeting, the internal affairs investigator was right behind him, thanking him for doing a wonderful job.

He spotted John, and flashed a smile. The detective exiting the meeting, didn't even seem to notice John as he slid past him with a blank stare, and continued down the hallway. Some of the detectives followed suit, and advanced down the hallway without speaking. Some took their place on the wall, waiting for their appointment times, John presumed.

They all seemed to have the same glazed look in their eyes, as if there was no life in them, and they didn't speak or acknowledge him. John wasn't one for conversation, so the silence suited him just fine.

"John Bigsby, you're up, come on in," the investigator said, "I'm Doug, and this is Bryan, we are both internal affairs investigators, and I'm sure you know this guy," Doug said, as he pointed to the Chief of Police who stood up, and walked towards John with an extended hand.

"Chief, of course," John said, as he gripped the Chief's hand tightly.

"Please, have a seat John," Doug said, as he pointed to the chair at the head of the long table, making John feel like a mafia don.

The Chief sat on one side, and the two investigators on the other. Doug took a sip of water, and got right to the point.

"There was a double homicide that you were the lead detective on." Doug said. "The scene was processed by you, and a few of the other detectives from your division. Unfortunately, your case has been compromised. Some of the evidence that was sent to the lab was tampered with by an officer, Joyce Anderson, who is no longer employed by this agency.

We are confident, that you can still solve this case, as you are one of the best; and you work with a team of detectives that are top notch. It is sad about what happened to those two young people, and the family is seeking closure, as is the rest of the city. They cannot rest at night knowing that a monster lurks among them. We need this case solved, and we need it solved pronto." Doug said.

Before John could respond, the other investigator, Bryan, spoke up.

"We have a few leads for you, we want to make sure that these names are investigated thoroughly, as they may have ties to some missing persons cases and, in your interest, some murders that have been discovered in the city.

We are putting together a task force that will begin taking out the trash in this city. You know what I mean?" Bryan said. "You have been chosen to assist with this initiative. You have a certain knack for solving cases, and you are one of the best. I guess you could say that you were born to do this."

The investigator chuckled, as he gave a conniving glance at the Chief. The Chief returned a knowing smile, as he spoke up.

"That's right Biggs, you were always destined to be a good detective, and I see big things in the future for you. You have always been a good steward, doing exactly as you were told, I mean trained."

The room fell silent.

"I am working with internal affairs to make sure that our great citizens of this city, our important clientele, are protected; and certain trash is removed from the street, so that everyone's future is protected here. We all have families, friends, and loved ones, that we want to ensure enjoy the peace and freedoms that we once knew. John, you are in the streets, in the trenches so to speak, and you see what is going on. The world is chaotic, and crime is out of control. Death is on the rise, and we need to start arresting and eliminating people who poison our society.

You will bring these animals to justice. You will be a part of something very big, and make a difference in the world. What you do is very important, never forget that. If you do exactly as we say, you will rise to the top, very quickly, and be a part of an initiative that will make the streets safe again.

Kids will be able to come out and play, people will be able to leave their doors unlocked again, police will be able to be a beacon of brilliance. Who knows, someday you could be my successor, the Chief! Hahaha, I want to retire someday," the Chief said with a wry laugh.

"Do you know what a monarch butterfly is, John?" the Chief asked rhetorically. "It is such a unique butterfly, because it can pass its abilities and strengths through genetics, to its future generations, and can produce several generations in just a few months. The other butterflies function the exact same way as all of its predecessors. The monarch is a lot like the family members of this police department.

Did you know, that during migration, monarchs cover thousands of miles with multi-generational return? They are everywhere, just like us. They have been around forever, just like us. There are many of them, just like us; for we are legion."

The Chief's voice seem to take on a deep, dark tone, as he narrowed his eyes at John.

"Like the monarch patriarch, I have passed on my knowledge to many of my subordinates, and I have reaped a great return. Your adopted father, Kyle Bigelow was one of those great subordinates. He was a great police officer, and his investigation skills were top-notch.

Although you are not his biological son, you too are very unique, and your skills are sharp and pristine; and exactly what this department has developed in you. You are smarter than he was. There are others just like you, and having a team comprised of the best of the best police officers, investigators, and detectives, makes us a very strong organization.

We are a brotherhood, a fraternal order. Your detective brothers have been together for a long time. They worked closely with your father, they will make sure that you are well taken care of, so listen to what they tell you. Remember, they work directly for me, and I am counting on your success, my young monarch.

You will continue to work with Detective Chris Kelley. He will fill you in as to exactly what you will need; he will continue to give you guidance. He may not always be there physically, but he will always be there if, and when, you need him. Here are the names that you may want to start with in your investigations."

The Chief took the paper that was handed to him by the investigator, and slid it over to John. At that moment, the door opened, and in walked a figure that John didn't notice right away, as he studied the paper that lie before him.

He finally looked up, and there sat Dark Man, staring across the table at John. John gripped the chair on both sides of the arm rests as he dug his nails into the cushion. His feet tensed up, and an overwhelming feeling of dread came over him as sweat beaded up and began to pool down John's forehead. John closed his eyes, not wanting to reveal his obvious fear to everyone in the room.

Dark Man began to whistle a familiar tune that made John open his eyes, which were now bloodshot. John felt a severe headache coming on, and knew that he was under complete submission. The whistling stopped, and words seared through John's eardrum, and erupted into his very soul.

"Hello John, are you ready to have a silent night?" Detective Kelley asked.

The evil, grotesque figure with the big yellow bulging eyes was replaced by Detective Chris Kelley as he sat in the chair next to the Chief.

"Make sure that he does not get out of line again," the Chief whispered quietly to Chris, who appeared like a hologram to John.

John looked across the table, and noticed the interfered pattern of Detective Chris that reflected Dark Man again, he grinned menacingly at John.

"I won't," he said, as John looked in horror.

Chapter 13

The police department was more than just a fraternal order; it was a family and a commitment. From the application process, to the grueling interview, to the eventual appointment to the police academy, each step tested the resilience and commitment demanded of each officer.

Even if it was just a thought process, the person knew what they were signing up for when deciding on a law enforcement career. Risks, danger, and death were top concerns, and one out of the three was sure to happen at any time during their career.

In the academy, the precedent was set early on for teamwork as bonds were formed. Each officer vowed to protect their fellow brothers and sisters in blue so that everyone would go home the same way they came.

Upstanding officers dedicated their lives for the job, often putting their safety on the line to protect property and people, who did not always appreciate their presence, due to a few bad apples. The few bad apples spoiled the whole bunch, ruining the adherence of the standards that great officers had set. Therefore, as a whole, the organization was tainted.

Good officers were often silenced, ridiculed, pressured, not provided backup, or fired if they spoke against the ill-intentions of their fellow brothers and sisters in blue. So, with their backs against the wall, and with society turning on them as they were grouped with crooked cops; good officers became burned out. The career they proudly signed up for, in-spite-of all of the baggage that came along with the badge, was now just a secure job that paid the bills, and provided for their families or lifestyles.

Officer Joyce Anderson felt that every time she put on her police vest, which once felt like a super hero cape, shielding her from all evil. However, the vest couldn't protect her from a broken heart, and the disappointment that was now cancerous to her mind; from the thought that her fellow brothers and sisters were not always doing the right thing.

Being on the force for all of those years gave her a perspective on life that almost gave her a third eye, as she was aware of things that few people could see. She knew that she was set up to take the fall for actions that she did not commit. It disappointed her, but did not surprise her.

She knew that it was not a third eye, but rather discernment, which she credited receiving from her Godly upbringing. With the risk of imminent danger or death always a handbreadth away, she knew better than to not have God on her side. She knew she always wanted to be a police officer, in hopes that someday she would make detective. She was always inquisitive as a little girl and asked lots of questions so she could get to the bottom of things with a clear understanding. Her mother and father were so patient and explained quite a bit to her about life. They spoke of injustices in the world, they spoke of good people and bad people, and they spoke of God, and gave her the upbringing that would shape her adulthood.

Equipped with the shield of faith, the breastplate of righteousness, and the helmet of salvation, she knew that she could best serve her community by vowing to protect and serve. She was a great police officer, who proved to be a quick study, and the job came naturally. She asked questions and got answers.

It was her knowledge that proved helpful to Officer Kyle Bigsby when they were rookies, freshly released to the streets. Whatever insight she could share with Kyle, she would, because Kyle was her partner. The streets responded to Joyce and trusted her. Informants gave her the information she needed to help solve the crimes, and she was sharp and smart. The upper management took notice of her deeds, and assigned her to tough areas, the areas that no one wanted to deal with. Paired with Officer Bigsby, they proved to be the best team on the department.

It was during those tough nights Joyce was able to witness to Kyle, who seemed to be losing his focus, as he was drawn into cliques that were formed at the department. He had moments when he was fun-loving Kyle, then there were moments when he seemed frustrated, distracted, and distant.

"What do you want most in life?" she asked him one night as they sat in their cruiser, eating hamburgers, with the ambience of a dark alley shrouding their vehicle.

"I just want to be happy, you know. I didn't have parents that were there for me, they never came to any of my football games, they never showed affection, and they never said, 'I love you, son.' They weren't at my graduation, and I really didn't have a plan in life after I crossed that stage. I thought about joining the military, the Marines. I figured it wouldn't be any tougher than what I went through for the 19 years I spent under their roof.

I was working out at the gym every day to get ready, and the Chief walked up to me one day. He worked out at the same gym. He asked if I had ever considered being a police officer. He took me under his wing, and I had never been accepted before. I stuck around him, met other police officers, and they showed me the ropes. I went to meetings with them until I was old enough to join the department, and here I am. But I'm still not happy, sometimes I feel controlled, like I don't have an identity or know who I am.

I see the worst in people, and it depresses me at times. Thank God I didn't join the military; I would probably feel worse. I just want a family; maybe a couple of kids to take to Disneyland, a wife to make love to, and who will hold me at night, and that's it. You know, the American dream, complete with the little house with the white picket fence, and a little dog."

Joyce listened intently, biting into her burger, chewing, and swallowing back the sadness that she felt for her friend. They sat quietly for a moment, with constant interruptions from the dispatcher that broke into the hush with radio traffic, only to return to dead silence.

Joyce finally spoke up. "Always trust God, Kyle. Put your trust in Him."

"You mean put my trust in someone that I have never seen, or who never did anything for me, when I suffered in silence at home for 19 years. Why would I do that?"

"Look at all this evil around us, Kyle. Can you even fathom how someone would take a machete, and with all of their might, bring it down on someone else's head until it split in half, knowing what that pain must feel like? Yet they do it anyway, with no regard. Would you say that person was evil to the core? Not human, a demon from the very pits of hell? Or do you think that humans are capable of such nasty, vile, unadulterated evil?

Well, I don't. I think it is an evil force from Hell, and if there is something that exists that makes a person behave in that manner, then there has to be a Heaven, there has got to be a God. I want whatever there is that is good to always be in my life, and a part of my life. Wouldn't you want that Kyle?

Even if it wasn't real, even if good and evil is just what we make it, I just want to think that there is good, and I will reap good things and will be rewarded in Heaven for my actions. Wouldn't it be a shame to find out that heaven and hell is real the hard way, when you can't do anything about it, except to be consumed by one or the other based upon your deeds?

I don't want to take a chance. I just gotta believe there is something good out there, I just want to believe in something good. I believe in God. Don't take a chance, Kyle. Trust in something; if you don't stand up for something, you will fall for anything."

Kyle wiped his mouth with his napkin, as he nodded his head, and looked over at Joyce.

"I got you to keep praying for me, right?" he said. "I will bow down to the mighty God someday, but today, I have to play God, and catch the bad guys."

Kyle cranked up the car, and put the spotlight on the alleyway as he slowly drove looking for a suspicious suspect in the area. It was the conversation they had before Kyle was snatched away by the good old boys in blue from another division. It wasn't long before he became the hero that rescued the little boy in the dilapidated apartment with his dead mother. Kyle got his wish, he became a father. Joyce did as she promised; she kept praying for him.

She never questioned the fact that a police officer would be allowed to adopt a child that was a part of an investigation, or that the Chief orchestrated the whole idea. She did, however, think that it was awfully strange that the Chief had his hand in it; especially when the streets kept her informed about the actions of her fellow police family. One of her informants confided in her.

"The police aint right," he told her. "I see what they are doing, they come around here at night, pick up young men off the streets, and then dump them back into the neighborhood. They are never the same when they come back, if they come back at all. I know what else they are doing; they are selling kids, they are selling organs, they are doping up our children, and sending them back to the streets, only to collect them later for their use. I know what they are doing, I may be homeless, and look like a crazy old man, but I'm not. I have been watching these streets for years. I know what I'm talking about. Just keep your eyes open, you'll figure it out," he told her.

She didn't discredit his information, but she knew his reputation for getting drunk, hallucinating, and passing out. She also knew that in the vicious cycles of his alcohol merry-go-round, that he was a good informant with a lot of useful information at times. She smiled as she remembered when he use to talk about the military tanks, equipment, and coffins, he would see traveling on the box cars of the trains that glided through late at night. Or the time that he claimed that he was Jesus, and that he had a message to give to the people about chemtrails that were poisoning the air.

"Conspiracy theorists are the most," she thought, as she shook the man's hand, and carried on with his theories about the police officers, in her back pocket.

Now she wondered how much of his drunken theories were true. She knew she had done nothing wrong. She did not deserve to be fired for something that she did not do. Her only recourse was to pray. She knew something was wrong, but she wasn't privy to information that explained the strange behaviors of her department.

"Dear Lord, I am broken, and my heart is in so much pain. You gave my mother Clara everything that she needed to survive the evil fate that surrounded her when she needed you the most. Now I ask for the same covering you gave to my parents, to encompass me with your love and protection, and reveal to me any evil that is present or trying to make its presence in my life, and defend and protect me. In Jesus name, Amen."

Chapter 14

John's reign of terror, was far from slowing down, he was gaining momentum with each assignment that he successfully completed. Although he had a list of suspects to investigate, he had a personal vendetta against one particular miscreant, an animal who had literally gotten away with murder.

John remembered arresting him on many occasions when he was a police officer patrolling the streets. He picked him up for drug offenses, home invasions, and notably a gang-related shooting in which he gunned down three men; two of whom were gang-members with an opposite agenda, but one was an innocent by-stander, a father of two who was at the wrong place, at the wrong time. John arrested him, delivered a few well-deserved blows to his face, and injected him with drugs on the way to the station. The man awaited trial, but escaped the murder charge on a technicality. After serving a little time for some drug offenses and burglary, he was back on the street.

John saw him one day as he was out perusing the neighborhood. The guy recognized John as well, and mocked him as he stood up from his illegal craps game, blowing him a kiss from the barrel of a gun configured of his thumb and index finger. John's knuckles turned white as he gripped the steering wheel so hard that his fingernails penetrated the faux leather steering wheel cover.

"Silent Night," pressed from John's pursed lips in a sinister rendition. "Tonight you belong to me!"

Once again the sudden onset of night covered the city, casting dark shadows, and hiding all discretions and guilty pleasures. For some it offered sleep, rest, and relaxation; for others, it afforded sins, secrets, and wickedness. It only allowed enough light to keep the world from total blindness; although it did not matter if it was day or night, the world was still afflicted with sightlessness. It is with this blindness that John could operate with ease, without being detected.

John passed the man in his car, and glared at him from his rearview mirror. He suddenly whipped the car around, as he noticed the man getting into position for a sprint to elude him. The chase led them down a street, where only a few boarded up houses remained, and dead-ended by a field riddled with broken bottles, old tires, and trash. The man, exhausted from running, turned around just before entering the dangerous grounds full of jagged glass, rebar, and nails, that were sure to impale him.

"What do you want, man?" the man said with his arms above his head. "I didn't do nothing."

John didn't speak, he turned out his headlights, exited the vehicle, and moved very quickly towards the man. He pulled a syringe from his jacket pocket and uncapped it, squirting some of the contents into the air.

"No man, no, what are you doing. Please stop!" the man screamed.

John prepared to stick the man in the side of his neck, but the man jumped back, wrestling his hand away. Only half of the contents were pushed into its objective, when John suddenly felt a burning sensation. He felt woozy, as he watched the man begin to act erratic and insane. It seemed as if he could see two, and then three versions of the man, writhing on the ground screaming. John could hear several voices, as he slowly fell to the ground himself. The voices sounded distorted and distant, as everything appeared like a mirage; and then John blacked out.

John woke up groggy; he felt a sharp pain in his leg, and looked down to see the syringe sticking out of his thigh, the needle pushed all the way in, until the tip of the syringe touched the skin. The needle sharply passed layers of tissue to release the contents that altered his personality, as he intended for his victim. He propped himself up on one arm and looked around to see that the man was gone; however, just a few feet away there was a body; bloody and eaten, as if someone gnawed the flesh off of his face, neck, and arms.

He couldn't comprehend what he was seeing, or what was happening to his body. He began to try to stand up, but he blacked out again, this time striking his head on the graveled pavement, his body lay quietly in the still of the night.

***

"Detective Bigsby, can you hear me? Detective open your eyes for me."

John woke up very groggy and confused. He jumped up to see if he was still in the same surroundings.

"Detective, calm down, we need for you to lie back down. You are in the hospital. Please lie down, Detective Bigsby. It's going to be ok." A nurse stepped into his view. "My name is Evan, I am the nurse on duty tonight. Can you tell me what happened?"

John tried to reach up to feel his head, realizing that he felt pain in the spot that was injured before.

"No, no, no, we don't need you reaching up there, you don't want to get anything infected," the calm and polite nurse said.

John's hair had already been shaved as the nurse prepared to stitch the open wound. Suddenly, the doctor whisked the curtain open, and quickly closed it as he entered into the tight space, staring at the back of John's head. His eyes widened, and he quickly opened his cell phone to place a call. Evan stood by, awaiting the order from the doctor to proceed with the job, as he dabbed the wound with a gauze soaked in saline solution to stop the blood that continued to seep from the wound and pour down the back of his head.

"Stop," the doctor demanded. "Nurse, I got it from here, I need you to excuse yourself please, and tend to the other patients. Thank you!"

The doctor suddenly spoke to the voice on the other end of the phone.

"Hey, we got one of yours. The end is in sight," the doctor announced, speaking in broken code.

John closed his eyes, and began to hum his programmed tune until he was unconscious.

Chapter 15

"**Babe,** babe, wake up. You gotta hear this. You will never believe what happened on my shift last night."

Joyce's eyes barely peeled open to find her husband hovering over her, waiting with child-like anticipation for her to respond.

"Evan, baby its 8:00 in the morning."

"I know, I tried to wait an hour or so but I couldn't. You have to hear about my night."

"Ok, ok, I'm up," Joyce said as she stretched, and adjusted her pillow to sit up and lean back on it.

"Ok late last night, a guy came into the hospital. He was a total mess, he was all bloody and half naked. It looked like someone had torn flesh off of his body, his face and neck were just hanging. He was like on an LSD trip or something, he couldn't be still. He was all over the place, screaming that he was hot, his eyes were wide, pupils dilated. He looked like he had seen a ghost.

It took a while, but he calmed down a little bit, which means he went from 100 to 98 on the crazy scale, right. So anyway, he finally says that someone tried to kill him. He just kept screaming it; someone tried to kill him. I asked him who, and he says a cop. So I was like, what cop, what is his name? He says, Bigsby, and he kept screaming it, Bigsby, Bigsby, Bigsby.

He says he injected him with something, and was trying to kill him. We ran tests on him, and kept him for observation. He didn't want to make a police report, he was afraid, and said the police were in on it. It took a few hours, but we finally got him calm, and rested, and then he was sent to the psychiatric wing."

Joyce sat up, staring at her husband, her hand over her mouth in disbelief.

"No wait, it gets better," Evan promised. "Hours later, we get an alert about an incoming unidentified male with head trauma, and possible fractures, and other injuries. So the ambulance pulls up, and it's none other than Detective Bigsby.

Now get this. He has a large gash in the back of his head, and he is bleeding like a stuck pig, so I get orders from the doctor to shave his head and prep him, so I can suture him up. When I shave his head, he has this symbol tattooed in the back of his head. I have never seen it before, so when no one was looking, I took a picture of it."

Evan pulled out his cell phone and proudly showed his wife the picture.

"It's a 5 pointed star and at every point are the letters O-R-D-E-R. In the middle of the star, it says C6. What the heck is that? C6 Order, sounds like a satanic secret society doesn't it? To top it all off, when the doctor came in, he immediately looked at the symbol and made me leave. It was weird."

Joyce's mouth opened even wider to match the size of her eyes, which she had to wipe numerous times, as she looked at the picture for confirmation of what she was seeing.

"C6 Order! I know what that is, my mom told me about it years ago," she said.

Joyce shook her head, as she covered her mouth again, and closed her eyes.

"Well, what is it? You're killing me," Evan said, as he looked at the picture again.

"Evan, the Chief had that same symbol on his wrist. It all makes sense now."

"What makes sense? Because right now, nothing you are saying makes any sense to me," Evan pounded the bed in frustration and anticipation.

"Evan, before I was born, my mom Clara worked for a preacher. He was the biggest mega preacher in the whole city. He was filthy rich; he had a TV show, a radio show, jets, everything that you can imagine, he had it. My mom was his assistant, and she told me that this secret group known as the C6 order approached the pastor.

They were very bad men, Evan. They controlled his every move, they inducted the pastor into their organization, and when he was in, everything totally changed. His ministry was no longer a godly ministry, it was now an agenda.

The C6 Order knew that people would always trust a pastor; and this church had a huge following. People wanted to believe in something good, and this pastor gave them hope. He spoke what they wanted to hear, and made them feel like they belonged in spite of the corrupt world they had to face every day which was not always so accepting.

The C6 Order wanted to push the agenda of a microchip to be placed under the skin of every person in the city. They eventually wanted to make it worldwide, but this was going to be the pilot program to start it.

Now of course, everyone was against it, because it made people think that it was the Mark of the Beast described in the Bible; 666, or a chip that allows the government to control and follow people. However, if they could get an influential pastor to say it was safe; not the mark, but simply a chip that would help people, help catch criminals, help people readily get medical attention and food, then they could introduce it with little to no resistance.

If they could get the pastor to convince people that it was ok, people would do it with no hesitation, because they trusted this pastor. So, it was decided the chip would be given to people in the congregation one Sunday, with promises of money to the first participants. The church was brand new, they were having a grand opening service, and the chip was going to be introduced. People came out by the thousands, and the church filled to capacity. The church filled so much that the Fire Marshal showed up.

Just as they got up to introduce the rfid chip, something happened. A transformer, or generator blew up, and caught fire. The people were so packed in they couldn't escape, and the sanctuary caught fire burning the building down with everyone inside. People blocked the entrance doors from the outside, because they were packed in the foyer trying to get inside. Those who couldn't get inside, finally realized what was happening, and some of them were able to escape; but sadly, most of them did not escape. It was a horrific event, very tragic; the pastor died. Members from C6, and other organizations showed up that day, lots of people, and they were all killed in the fire.

No one heard from the C6 Order, or anything else about the chip again. My mom didn't go to the church that day, she survived. She told me all about this organization and she described this symbol, which is this very symbol that you are showing me now. If they are here in Texas, they are everywhere. Evan we are in trouble if C6 is now a part of the police department."

Joyce pulled back the covers, and walked back and forth, frantically looking for clothes to put on.

"Where are you going?" Evan asked, still processing the story.

"I have to talk to someone, one of my informants. I haven't talked to him in some time, but he used to try to tell me about the police, and I thought maybe he was just a conspiracy nut, but now I think he can help me put some things together. I have to talk to him."

"Babe, wait! You are no longer a police officer. You can't go into these neighborhoods without the protection of the badge you once had. It gave you the authority to be there, now you have no place going down there talking to people." Evan said.

"I have the protection from the Lord, Evan! That is my badge. It's praying time, Evan, its praying time more than ever before. We have to let God protect and serve." She stopped for a moment just to kiss her husband's forehead. "I have God on my side," she said with confidence. "Now get some sleep, I will be back to cook your favorite meal this evening; lasagna, a nice salad, some garlic knots, and great sex for dessert!"

"Ha, ha, ha! Well, I'll sleep to that," he said, as she slipped away to the bathroom to shower.

***

Armed with a BBQ sandwich and a soda, Joyce set out to find the homeless man everyone deemed crazy. She had not seen him in years. She was worried he may be dead after living on the streets for so long, nourished by bottles of cheap wine, and fast food when he could get it.

She drove through the neighborhood, which had seen better days, for it looked worse than before, with its boarded buildings, and broken down homes. Dogs roamed the streets, and people walked around in despair. She noticed the homeless sitting with their backs against a brick building, the walls decorated in gang graffiti, its sidewalk with scattered broken glass.

She stuck her head out the window and screamed, "Has anyone seen the Sandman?"

"Nope," one of them said, laughing more than necessary.

"Maybe, I have seen him, but it will cost you for that information," another one said.

Joyce continued to drive down streets, underpasses, parks, everywhere she thought he could be. Fearing the worst, she turned her car into the parking lot of an old car wash no longer in operation, and parked the car to strategize her next move. She suddenly noticed a man lying on the ground in one of the car stalls. He was barefoot, with tattered clothes that barely covered his thin frame, revealing ribs that pressed through thin skin. Joyce got out of the car, and carefully walked over to the man, who was coughing and lying in the fetal position, despite the sunny day.

"Sandman?" she said.

"Leave me alone, what do you want?" he asked, clutching his clothes and holding on to himself even tighter.

"Sandman, it's me Officer Joyce Anderson. I want to help you."

"Go away," he insisted.

"You're sick, I have food, and I can get you some medicine. Come on, come with me," she said reaching out her hand to him. "It's going to be OK, I am going to help you."

The man looked up with eyes that had seen years of things that made them sunken and sad. They were watery and red, a look of exhaustion made them dark. He reached up his hardened hand, caked with years of dirt. As Joyce assisted him to his feet, the smell almost made her fall to her knees. She led him to her car anyway, and carefully put him in the back seat.

"I'm going to get you some medicine," she said, as she pulled away from the parking lot and raced for a drugstore.

He did not answer. Joyce looked back and saw the man was slumped over, and appeared to be asleep. Joyce pulled into a drugstore, bought cough syrup, and then drove to a hotel where she went inside and made arrangements for an extended stay.

She got him inside, and uncapped the cough syrup, putting the bottle to his lips, pouring the contents into his mouth, which he swallowed like a fifth of his favorite liquor. She gave him the food, which he gobbled down. He wiped his mouth with the back of his hand, and sat on his bed, staring at Joyce, who sat at a desk positioned by the window of the cheap hotel.

"What do you want, with me? I'm a sick old man, just leave me alone and let me die," he said with a raspy, phlegm-filled voice.

"Sandman, I want you to rest. When you wake up, and feel up to it, I want to talk to you about the bad things that the police did."

"Ha, ha, ha," he responded, laughing which soon gave way to a coughing fit. "Why, do you want to talk about the police? You don't believe anything about them anyway. Just leave me alone, I say. I just want to die now."

"What do you know about the C6 Order?" she asked.

The man stopped laughing, and looked at her again quietly, this time his facial expression showed seriousness and fear.

"I know everything," he said.

The man laid back on the bed to get comfortable. He looked up at the ceiling, and began to recall everything in his brain pertaining to the Order.

"You can laugh at me if you want to girl, but I know what's going on."

"I promise, Sandman, I won't laugh. I believe you, I need to know what's going on. I'm not a police officer anymore." Joyce said.

Sandman turned his head slightly to look at her, and then turned back to stare at the ceiling once again.

"Oh, you finally wised up huh, girl? It's about time, it's never too late to come to your senses," he chuckled.

"Sandman, please," she said.

"They plan to turn everyone into zombies. Not the zombies that you see on TV, either, but the idea will be the same. They will be the walking dead, not able to think for themselves or do for themselves, and will be a danger to society, worthy of incarceration or death.

The rest of them, the upper echelon, have protected themselves by making serums and vaccinations from our strong, rich blood, and the blood from strong animals that have endured temperature extremes, poisonous bites, and intelligence. They have studied the genes and DNA from the best of the best animal, plant, and human species to protect them from the serums and vaccinations that they have given everyone else. They have secret bunkers in locations all over the world. When the order is given, they will flee, leaving us to die."

"How do you know this?" Joyce asked.

"I am smarter than people give me credit for."

The man began to get a little strength in his body as he sat up on the side of the bed, and took a sip of water from the bottle on the night stand beside him.

"I was kidnapped when I was young teenager. You see, at that time I was in a gang, and me and my homeboys at that time were into all kinds of stuff. We were breaking the law, fighting, stealing, and robbing. We were doing everything that you can think of, and we were about to go to jail.

One day a task force rounded all of us up, threw us in a van, and threatened to put us away for a long time; or we could come with them, and they would let us go when they were done. We thought they were going to interrogate us, get us to snitch about something, rough us up a bit, and then let us go.

They blindfolded us, and drove us somewhere that took us a long time to get to. They attached things to our bodies, and then put us in individual little rooms. It was pitch black in the rooms; you couldn't see your hand in front of your face. The rooms must have been sound proof, because we couldn't hear each other, even though we were yelling out for each other.

They came and got us after a couple of hours. They were wearing lab coats, and they led us to another room that was like a movie theatre, but the seats had straps on them. They strapped our arms and legs to the chairs. We were made to watch a video; it wasn't long, it showed words that went across the screen. Words like kill, animal, torture, death, guilty, assassin. Then the video showed good words like, God, trust, believe; I can't remember all of the words.

They would deliver shocks to our bodies, it was so excruciatingly painful, that we thought we were going to die. Then the video started showing genocide, homicide and carnage. If we looked away, we were shocked. If a good word flashed across the screen, we were shocked. Then we were led back to the dark room.

This went on for days. We lost our sense of time, and space, and depth perception, it was strange. We felt like we were nonexistent. We were starved during that time. I don't know how long it lasted, but we finally got food, and then the next day no food, no videos, just darkness.

Suddenly through speakers in our rooms we heard the words being spoken that we saw on the video; kill, animal, guilty, assassin. After hearing that all day in a loop, we were led back to the theatre room. We were all so scared because we knew that the shocks were coming. We suddenly heard a man's voice.

'Subject #1, do you believe in God?'

My homeboy answered, 'Yes, yes I do.'

He was shocked, I still hear his shrieks as the volts surged through his body. The voice came across again,

'Subject #2, do you believe in God?'

Subject #2 answered no, and he was immediately given food.

Subject #3, #4, #5; all of us knew to say no. We were all given food to eat. They then told us that we were powerful, we were invincible and strong, and that we could withstand anything. They gave us each a word that we were instructed to remember. They blindfolded us and put us back in the van, took us back to our neighborhood, and dumped us out. Everyone, except my homeboy that answered yes, that he believed in God.

We never knew what happened to him, none of us ever talked about what happened. We feared the shocks would come again. I think they planted something in our bodies, something was put in my teeth. I could hear those voices talking to me through it. They would tell us to kill; if we didn't, we got headaches that were almost worse than the shocks.

One of my partners went on a mass shooting spree, killing more than 30 people in a shopping mall, and then took his own life. One was a big time drug lord, he was responsible for bringing the drug Fleek into the city. He was called an animal in the news when he made a full confession, and admitted to all kinds of terrible crimes. He's in prison right now, in lockdown, solitary confinement. He only sees the daylight for an hour each day. Everyone else is either in prison or dead now.

My headaches were so bad that I pulled out one of my molars to make the voices stop. You know what I found? A tiny little device the size of a pencil tip and it had wires coming from it. I knew no one would believe me.

I went to the emergency room once because I got very sick, a doctor walked in, and when he saw me, he began to say those words to me from the video that was shown to us. He was there at that place, because he knew my word. I left, ran as fast as I could and never went back. I became homeless, sick, and according to everyone that I tried to tell this story to, crazy."

The old man paused to take a breath and collect himself.

"I have watched from the sidelines, over the years; kids and adults being kidnapped. I have seen people being killed, I have seen all kinds of things that you would not believe that goes on when people don't think they are being watched. I watched one day as a van pulled into an alley, and the mysterious men inside dropped a wooden box, right smack in the middle of the alley, and then drove away into the night.

It wasn't long before some young boys started snooping. They worked hard at it, but they finally got that lid off that box. I suddenly saw black metallic guns of all kinds, glistening against the moon. Who drops a box full of guns in a neighborhood full of kids? These guns weren't even street legal, you can't go to a store and find these guns; but there they were, in the hands of teenagers, who distributed them. That drop of weapons, started a war in this community. I have never seen so much murder in my life.

It was the same kind of van that picked up me and my partners years ago. This community is still feeling the effects of that drop.

One young guy that lived on the streets with us said he was in and out of juvenile detention. He said that the kids there are being brainwashed. It doesn't matter the race, the gender, or the age, they were shocking kids who didn't behave.

Girls were being raped, and turned out, and once they left juvie, they were sold into sex trafficking and prostitution rings. I watched police officers pick up kids, and when they returned to the streets, they were different. They were either zombies or wild animals. Where were the parents you ask? Good question. Something bad is happening, Ms. Anderson. Find our missing."

The man fell back on the bed, and rolled over to his side with his back to Joyce. Soon after, he curled up into the fetal position, and began to snore.

Joyce put the bottle of cough syrup on the nightstand with the water. She went out, and returned with a few groceries to sustain him for a few days, and whispered,

"Thank you, Sandman," as she quietly closed the door behind her, leaving her sleeping friend to his moments of peace and quiet, in a nice warm bed for a change.

"Dear Lord, please protect us from the dogs, the evildoers, those mutilators of the flesh."

She knew that she had work to do.

Suddenly, at that very moment, there was a great move in the Heavens, as God assembled his angels. There appeared a beacon of light, hope, and love that burned in the spirits of all of the angels, and all mankind who were in tune, and praying at that needed moment.

Although the storms of life were manifesting, brewing, and stirring fear in all of the inhabitants of its destructive path, there was a certain calm amidst the storm. Praying people were fearless, they realized there needed to be a shift in the atmosphere. Prayers lit up like small beams of light, extending to the heavens, until the Earth appeared like a beacon of billions of flickering flames.

"Listen to them," God said, as the angels bowed their heads in reverence.

"They need me, they love me, and they are calling upon me. The sounds of their prayers and cries for mercy are like sweet melodies that overflow, spilling like a fresh renewing rain on a warm dawn. Take your positions. It is time."

Chapter 16

"*The* time has come," the Chief said to his soldiers in the barn, hidden from humanity. The wooded area was a perfect cover for the old barn that appeared abandoned, cold, and run down. Inside it was a well-organized operation that held the best and the brightest minds in the state. Scientists, doctors, politicians, teachers, law enforcement officials, they were all in attendance, listening intently to the man who spoke eloquently at all of their meetings concerning the next move to improve the city; and with collaborations everywhere, the world.

"You are here today because you are leaders. You have all done well, and because of your efforts, Operation Street Sweep is about to be a huge success. We have all of our willing servants in place. We, the members of the C6 Order, will carry out our assignment to rid the world of the unwanted, and restore the natural selection of this land. Dr. Fleising, please inform the Order of what is being done."

"Bring the children," the doctor said, as he held out his hand to one of his assistants. Children were led into the middle of the circle, blindfolded, but very compliant and robotic.

"Subject #1," the doctor said, as he removed the blindfold from a little girl. "I want to know what your mission is."

The little girl wiped her eyes, and looked around the room.

"I am to be a good girl, and do what I am told."

"Yes, you are a good girl, I am so pleased with your progression," the doctor said. "Now go over and kill Subject # 2. Be a good girl and do what you are told."

Instantly, the little girl lost the life in her eyes, became robotic, immediately walking to subject #2 who was still blindfolded, removing a knife from her pocket.

"Stop," the doctor said, "What do you think you are doing?" The little girl began to cry.

"Was I bad, doctor?" she asked with a whimper.

"No honey, you were not bad, go with the nice nurse so that she can give you, and your friends, some treats. How does that sound?"

The doctor motioned for one of his assistants to take the children away.

"Do you all see what happened? She had no idea that she was preparing to do something so heinous. She has not been hypnotized, or brainwashed. She simply followed a command as it was given to her. It was like second nature, like she was doing what she was supposed to do. Or what she was told to do, by her dominant.

Much like the Jewel Wasp. Ah! The Jewel Wasp, quite a beautiful insect. The Jewel Wasp is found in parts of Africa and Asia; but what makes this creature so interesting, is its mind control capability. It renders its victim useless, and the female practically turns its victim into a mind-controlled puppet.

Her venom is first injected into the legs of a cockroach to paralyze it, and then venom is injected into the nerve center, or the brain of the cockroach. The cockroach is then in a compliant state, where it can be controlled. The wasp then drags the roach by its antenna, into its lair, and lays her egg on the roach's belly. The larva then begins to eat the roach, who is still in a state of control, unable to do anything about it.

The Costa Rican Wasp, Hymenoepimecis argyraphaga; acts in a similar manner. You see, the Costa Rican wasp injects venom into its host; in this case, the Orb Spider, rendering it useless. It forces the spider to do extraordinary things, like spin a web that it has never been able to spin before; it is the spider's best work. The female wasp lays an egg on the spider, and it injects a chemical into it, zombifying the spider.

This Orb Spider begins spinning that web with persistence, with such majesty and glory. However, the web is not for the spider. Instead, the spider is used so that the larva can suck it dry, killing it. The larva can now thrive, able to withstand anything in such a wonderfully built web.

For years, people have been injected, so to speak, with neurotoxins that have rendered them useless. It wasn't in the vaccines and flu shots like people were led to think."

Everyone in the barn began to laugh, as they looked at each other, shaking their heads at the ignorance of conspiracy theorists.

"What is the most commonly consumed food product in the world?" he asked.

Everyone looked around, some whispered to each other, what they thought it could be, but the doctor interrupted and loudly proclaimed the answer.

"It is corn. Corn is the most consumed food product worldwide. It has so many uses, and is used to make so many other food products. It can be used to make cornstarch, flour, gluten, oil, fibers, etc. The list goes on.

There is an even longer list of products that *use* corn, like antibiotics, aspirin, baby food, beer, candy, coffee, and tea. Developments were made so that we could modify corn that would protect itself, and produce a better product that would be beneficial for everyone, but we could also modify the corn to alter the course of our very existence. Now I will turn it over to a scientific expert, to help break this down in layman's terms, so you can understand our objectives from here. Dr. Fritz, please come."

The doctor dramatically stretched his hand out, giving the scientist the platform.

"I will try my best to break this down for you, so that I don't get too scientific, and lose my audience. What we are doing is so important, and you will understand why it was necessary to take the course that we took to ensure that we, as a people, are safe," Dr. Fritz proclaimed.

"We are the wasp, as the good doctor here has described. We are here to protect the other wasps, so to speak, and sometimes that can mean that nature does its job of natural selection, so that the strong survive and carry on the strength of the world.

That being said, corn is a widely used product that has been around for centuries; it is also an excellent product for genetic engineering. Our goal has been to combine genetic material from any species so that we could transfer genetic material between species that would never interbreed in nature. For instance, transfer of human genes into animals, or genes from a dog transferred into a cat. We have experienced some extraordinary breakthroughs in early studies of this process.

Well, if we could transfer genetic material between species, we could do that same thing with corn, and other food for that matter. Now, I know you are thinking that this is impossible, there are barriers that prevent this from happening; but what if we were able to *do* the impossible. What if we could combine viruses and bacteria from different sources, grow them in a lab, and transfer them into humans, plants, and animals? This could be accomplished in the same manner in which we were able to combine genetic material in species that would never breed in nature.

It is far more technical and scientific than this, but here is what we have found when we studied the corn experiment," Dr. Fritz continued.

"We have been conducting this testing for many years. We created a modified corn that could sustain itself against herbicides, temperature extremes, and other damage. We fed this corn to pigs, and they became stronger, more resilient, and more active for a while, and then they became more violent and crazed, mauling each other, until they eventually died. The gene altering of the corn coupled, with the genes that were gleaned from the pigs was then tested so that we could know the effects on people."

Dr. Fritz took a brief pause, and continued on.

"We discovered that in people, they were developing sicknesses, diseases, and psychological problems with this version of the corn. So we went back to the lab, and altered some things, but this time we decided to test the new product on inmates.

We put the genes into maltodextrin, which is made from corn, which is then used in coffee granules to keep them free-flowing. We also put it in the powdered coffee cream, which is made of artificial corn product, and we introduced these products into the prison system. What we found was that the inmates were stronger, faster, more aggressive, and their testosterone was through the roof. It was extraordinary.

However, after long term use, the inmates lost cognitive function, suffered memory loss, and most of all they could be controlled by the guards, because they didn't have a clear thought process, and seemed to lose the fight they once had. The prison system truly benefitted from this, as the assaults and aggressive behavior drastically decreased.

We slowly released this modified corn product into society, and over the years we were getting the same effects; developmental problems, memory loss, and aggression, but astounding strengths and abilities. We studied children from all over the world, bringing them into our labs, studying their organs, testing their blood; following and charting their development, growth, and activity throughout their life cycle."

The scientist's eyes changed into black mirrors of evil as he spoke.

"Here is the part that you will find interesting. After much testing, with trial and error, we have harnessed that aggression, strength, and energy for our use. We introduced a vector in the maltodextrin in some of our subjects, and we were essentially able to make mind-controlled super assassins equipped to kill our enemies. They could be used to find criminals, to seek out terrorists, and take out our foes in war.

We used runaways, inmates, detainees, criminals, and other participants, very much like the wasp uses the cockroach. They were willing to do anything that we needed them to do. Like the wasp, after it has finished making the cockroach or the spider, in our scenario do exactly as it wants, it sucks them dry, and then it simply flies away, leaving a dying carcass.

What does all of this mean for you who stand in this room, the elite? We have saved the best for last, or in our case, the best for the first! We have harnessed the best qualities from these cockroaches for ourselves."

Everyone began to laugh.

"Raise your glasses gentlemen, and drink the life-force that gives us power and dominion, for we are the wasps," the scientist said, as he lifted a champagne flute filled with the thick red substance that would intoxicate them with giddiness.

The scientist lowered his glass, removing a white handkerchief from his pocket, to wipe his lips.

"For far too long people have populated this Earth, and have not contributed anything viable into our society, our environment, our advancement. Our law enforcement can attest to the increase in crimes that affect innocent people. Teachers, you are finding that in the classrooms, kids are not learning anything that will cause them to grow up and use that knowledge for the productivity of our existence. They are like zombies in the classroom. Doctors, you see the diseases and ailments costing billions of dollars each year. Politicians, we are threatened with attack on our soil, and imminent wars throughout, as our enemies greedily hold on to minerals, resources, fuels, money, and oil that can greatly enrich the Earth.

This must stop, otherwise our future generations will suffer global warming, overpopulation, and martial law. This beautiful world we live in will turn into a desolate wasteland, if we don't put our foot down."

Everyone shook their heads in agreement, as their eyes too, began to gloss over and turn black. Their shadows, displayed by the light cast down from above, revealed large demon-like figures.

"We studied the strength and resilient qualities of human, plant, and animal species, and have gleaned the perfected qualities of each, making genetic material that protects us from the harmful effects we have introduced to the rest of the world.

Did you know that ants survive extreme conditions, and can carry three times their weight? They are able to live underwater for up to 24 hours. Camels are built for survival. They can live for six months without a meal, and a month without water, and they too can withstand extreme temperatures and conditions. The Emperor Penguin endures the worst conditions on Earth. They see no sun for four months, and sometimes find it difficult to find any food at all.

Now my favorite, the tardigrade. The tardigrade, *Hypsibius dujardini*, is a microscopic invertebrate, and the most resilient of them all. In a state of cryptobiosis, they are difficult to kill because they need no food or water. They can survive in zero degree temperature or up to 151* C. They can withstand 1,000 times more radiation than any other animal, and can tolerate very high levels of environmental toxins. They can even survive in outer space.

The genes of the Tardigrade, and all other genes of strength and ability from humans, animals, and plant subjects, introduced into a parasite, are perfect vectors for horizontal gene transfer.

We have harvested the organs and blood products of people from every race, all over the world, people with amazing strength, ability, wisdom, and resilience. Some of us, right now, carry within our bodies organs from the best of the best donors. Slow programmable freezing has allowed us to preserve the perfect gene, and with this gene we have developed a serum for ourselves. With the power of this gene transfer, we have made something so powerful we are able to withstand any condition, any extreme, and any medical disability that would befall any man; we are invincible."

Dr. Fritz paused for effect, letting the information sink in.

"At a designated time, the gene will be activated that has lain dormant in the cells of all the other people who have consumed the corn product that we altered. The immune system will respond to this infection, which will in turn activate the dormant genes. Once the dormant gene is activated, people will go crazy, turning on themselves, destroying each other, acting like zombies, and we will have complete control over them. They will eradicate themselves, creating a purge effect that will clear out the undesirables of the world.

Only those who have stayed away from such products, which is only 10 percent of our population, and have taken the serum will be safe from the harmful effects sure to depopulate the world. We will be ridded of the weak, wounded, diseased, poor, and criminals; once they are removed, all that will be left will be the elite, to restore the planet to a natural, thriving, harmonious existence."

Everyone began to cheer, and patted each other on the back, smiling so that the corners of their lips stretched back to their ears like the joker, revealing a maniacal sneer. They looked on wildly as the drink took its effect on them, causing them to hallucinate. The Police Chief reclaimed his position at the front of the group.

"Gentlemen, we have an intricate city beneath the Earth, already prepared and ready. It is stocked with food, medicine, weapons, and transportation, enough to sustain us for many years, if need be. I am told that it is absolutely beautiful and vast. When the cue is given, we will head to the secret location and live a thriving existence in our new home as we await the purging of this wretched society. Afterward, we can began the gentrification of our neighborhoods, our cities, our towns, our world!"

The Chief smiled with delight, as everyone clapped and cheered with extreme pleasure.

John stood in the shadows of the barn, listening to the proceedings, his head bandaged, and the weakness overtaking him. In the wild merriment, the Chief walked away from the revelers towards John, who attempted to move back into the darkness, so as not to be seen.

"You should go lie down, John, you're not well. Go with the doctor, he will take care of you," the Chief said with a smile. John began to feel dizzy, as his legs trembled and wobbled, as he stood looking at the Chief.

The doctor approached the two of them, and assisted John through a breezeway of horse stalls now transformed to small surgical suites and rooms. They continued the long walk out of the barn area to another building that looked like a storage facility with its individual rooms and dim lights. A door was opened, leading to a small hospital bed inside.

"Get in bed, John," the doctor spoke as he drew up medication to ease John's pain. "This will help you rest."

John instantly felt very groggy, sleepy, and unable to speak. His eyes blinked rapidly, fighting to stay awake. He saw the white lab coat of the doctor fading away with each flutter of his eyelids. He finally closed them, unaware of his allies' activities.

Chapter 17

A news brief, temporarily halted the regularly scheduled program on television. Everyone in the bar groaned, as it disrupted the most important football game of the season, during a critical play.

"That's bullshit!!" one of the patrons yelled out.

"Yeah, they do that to cause a riot, what the Hell!" another demanded.

They all began to order more beer, yell, and complain, as they threw pretzels and food items at the mounted televisions placed throughout the bar. They complained so much that they missed the news brief explaining that there appeared to be a massive amount of deaths in the area. A spokesman for the Center for Disease Control took the platform and explained to everyone who listened that there was a high death count for people catching the flu, and that precautions should be taken.

"What we can tell you is that this strain of flu is not like any others that we have seen before. This flu virus has combined with genes from other viruses in the past to cause recombination. This new flu is showing some drastic effects, there have been reports of high fever, cold sweats, disorientation and confusion. Please, we urge everyone to wash your hands thoroughly, cover your nose and mouth when you cough or sneeze, and try to stay home if possible. Thank you," the CDC official announced.

The game suddenly returned, and all the intoxicated patrons cheered and returned to their intense game watching and play calling, unaware of the horrors taking place outside of the bar in the chill of the night.

On this night, John found himself sitting in a vehicle, with its illegally tinted windows, right beside the Chief, who did his best to explain his intentions for John's allegiance. They were surrounded by darkness, exposed to the creatures of night.

"Biggs, you were chosen while you were very young, handpicked to carry out law enforcement duties. You have done well, and I am proud of your accomplishments. You remind me a lot of me. I guess you could say that you are me, and I am you.

It is because of your faithful duties that I have allowed you to join me in the C6 order. Our Order has been a part of a great initiative. We have acquired women, men, and children in the name of science, so that their organs and blood could be studied, used, and placed in viable hosts. People will use these new and improved transplants for something productive as they work to create a better society and way of life. Your initiative was to kill."

John looked over at the Chief in horror, as he didn't realize the man knew every move he made.

"You were bred and born to kill, and then find suspects that you could blame for these murders. It created a ruse so that the C6 order could hide; excuse me, I mean, continue their business of selling people for parts. People hid in fear of serial killers, when the real killers stood before them with a badge. Hahaha…" the Chief laughed dryly.

"Don't worry, you helped to convict people who had already committed crimes for which they were not caught. You did nothing wrong, you simply cleansed the Earth of these undesirables. The people you killed were just a part of the circle of life.

I have been informed by people much higher up, and with a much higher pay grade than me or the C6 Order, that the flu going around is the beginning of the end. This flu is bad enough, but the new strain that is coming is devastating. People will develop a high fever, they will suffer memory loss, they will become extremely aggressive and they will lose brain function. What's more, this virus will prevent the brain from processing serotonin, which keeps us all calm.

People will practically turn into zombies, attacking and killing each other; they won't be able to control it. Here is what is funny: people already kill each other over shoes, over the latest cell phone or video game. Hell, they even kill each other over turf that doesn't even belong to them. Why do you think that is?" the Chief asked.

"It's because they want things; they want status, they want money, they want success, and they think success lies in material things. People are so consumed by what they see on social media, television, and in music, that they think this is the way to wealth and success. After all, they see their favorite actor, singer, and law makers, enjoy wealth and power; media has full control of them. Of course, their minds are already controlled with genetically modified food, prescription drugs, illegal drugs, and pollutants pumped into the air. People are experiencing depression, mental illnesses, diseases, psychological problems, cancers, memory loss; all kinds of shit; and they are easily influenced and controlled.

People are turning into mindless zombies, killing each other over next to nothing already. We have already stung their front legs, like the Jewel Wasp. What do you think will happen when we turn it up a notch; when we paralyze their brains?"

The chief gave John a look, as if waiting for a response, and continued.

"When this new strain of flu is introduced, people will start to get sick, they will see people dying from it by the droves, and will run out to get vaccines that will pretty much be useless against this strain.

Now listen to this; as people start dying from the flu, it will create a panic on social media and on the news, the fastest way to spread information. People will run out to the stores to buy up supplies of food and water so they can stay at home for protection. Weapons will be grabbed from every shelf to defend their homes, life, and property. No one will want to go to work, or church, or any public place for fear of contracting the flu.

This will hurt the economy. Trucks will stop delivering food; and soon food, water, electricity, and other resources will begin to deplete all over the world, creating mass hysteria. Because of the panic, and sheer terror, the virus will spread very quickly. They will kill each other, mindless zombies. But we will be long gone, we will be safe from all of this, we are the elite."

John sat in silence and reached up to feel the back of his head that was still bandaged, as he made a revelation.

"But, I drank the coffee. Am I one of the mindless idiots that you spoke of?"

"What? No John, don't worry about that. I would never let you be harmed. You are fine, you are one of us." The Chief reassured him. "I will let you know when it is time to be mobile, it will not be long. You have already been injected with the necessary serum to keep you safe from the flu virus. Go home and rest, until it is time."

Suddenly something caught the Chief's eye. He didn't speak, which caused John to take notice as well. They noticed a man walking down the sidewalk dragging his feet and lumbering clumsily. He ran right into a trash can placed on the edge of a lawn for pick up the following morning. Although he tripped and fell, he slowly and awkwardly stood to his feet and continued his journey. A few feet away, they noticed a woman retrieving groceries from the back of her vehicle. They noticed the crazed man set his sights on the woman as he began to move rapidly toward her. The Chief quickly jumped out of the car.

"Hey," he said, calling out to the man.

The man paid him no attention, and quickly made it to the woman, who did not realize that she was in danger, as her head was buried in the trunk, grabbing at groceries that had shifted toward the back. The man grabbed her, and began biting at the back of her neck, as she screamed in terror. He overtook her, forcing her to the ground, and began gnawing at her face and neck relentlessly.

The Chief approached the man cautiously, giving orders for the man to stop or he would be shot. The man never looked up, as the Chief pulled his weapon and fired a shot into the man's back, which caused the man to spin around and set his sights on the Chief. His cold distant stare and hunched over gait scared the Chief who fired three more rounds into the man's body. The man fell over onto the ground beside the woman, who was shrieking hysterically. People began to come out of their houses.

"Bath salts," someone yelled out. "I bet it's bath salts, it's getting out of control."

John was already on the radio getting more units into the area, and it wasn't long before every available law enforcement official was on the scene. The same crew showed up as usual; every news anchor was setting up cameras and positioning themselves to capture the events of the evening. Paramedics were on the scene, as well as crime scene technicians, and detectives. The Chief and John returned to the vehicle.

"Bath salts?" John asked.

"No," the Chief looked worried, as he shook his head in disbelief. "I was told this happened at least 10 times tonight in other parts of the city. We have to do what we have to do to protect people, even if that means discharging our weapon. Stay vigilant, looks like things are progressing rapidly.

They quietly drove away from the scene.

***

"Hey babe, what are you doing?"

"I am at home, watching the news, can you believe how bad this flu epidemic is getting?" Joyce said to her husband.

"Great, I am glad that you are at home, the hospital has been swamped. People are getting sick, I have never seen it like this. I want you to stay at home babe, please don't go out, it seems to be spreading faster than people think. They are calling it the Z-flu now, zombie flu, because it seems to be making people turn into zombies. They are not announcing that name to the public. Do you know what will happen if the news was to say the word zombie? Oh my God, people would lose their minds."

"Where did you get the name Z-flu from?" Joyce inquired.

"I don't know," Evan said, "I made it up, I think. Or I may have heard someone say it, but I'm not positive, it's been crazy around here. According to the CDC it's just Influenza. Just stay home babe, I don't want to take a chance of you getting sick."

"I won't go anywhere Evan, but I want you to be careful. You are up there in the middle of all this."

"I'll be fine, you know your man is strong," he joked.

After all that Joyce had heard and seen, she knew this was a much dire situation than people realized. She knew she had to do something more than just sit on the couch. She called the one person that she knew could get a prayer through, her mom, Clara. She picked up the phone and used her words carefully, as she never wanted to let on about how things were going since her mother worried about her taking a law enforcement role.

"Hey ma, how are you and dad doing?"

"Oh honey, we are doing wonderful. It is so good to hear from you. How are you doing? Are you staying safe?"

"Always ma, always. The flu is pretty bad down here, a lot of people are dying. It is out of control." Joyce said.

"We have been down this road before my dear. We are not worried or afraid. We are always prepared, you know that we have relied on homeopathic remedies, and most of all God, and we always turn out just fine. I hope that you and Evan have been taking your supplements, and eating the right foods, fresh organic fruits and vegetables."

"Yes mom, of course. Between you and Evan, I am a walking nutrition zombie" Joyce laughed.

How is the job, honey?" Clara asked, concerned.

"Things are going to be good now mama, I have laid down my badge, and I am about to step into a leadership role," Joyce said, waiting to hear the excitement in her mom's voice.

"Honey, that is wonderful. I always told you that you would be a great leader someday, and that you would influence many lives and help many people. Always trust God, put Him first in everything; as you lead, let Him lead, and the gates of hell shall not prevail against you."

"I will, mama. I just had to hear your voice, to remind me that everything was going to be alright."

"Of course, my dear, everything is going to be alright. Lord, do on earth as it is heaven, in my favorite girl's life," Clara said, whispering a prayer on Joyce's behalf.

Joyce hung up the phone and smiled. Leaving the role of police officer was a great transition, she knew her mom worried about her being on the streets. She knew that what she was going to do now would be something meaningful and impactful. She would influence a much-needed change in the city.

Chapter 18

John sat quietly in his cold, dark kitchen. He had not returned to work in weeks. The Chief gave him some time off to recover. It was the only time the streets were safe from his atrocities but unfortunately, evil never rested, it just transferred, and killings continued to haunt the city. John coughed up blood, and the crimson sputum plopped onto the table below. He could not seem to beat the sickness that had suddenly overcome his body, and he feared that he was the victim of the heinous acts that were supposed to be purported for the less than in society.

His headaches kept him in a constant state of mania, and he could think of nothing other than the pain in which he seemed to be trapped. He also hallucinated, seeing Dark Man, in and out of his conscious. He could see and hear the Chief, the scientists, and the doctor in the corner of his kitchen, explaining the maniacal plan the higher elites concocted. He watched them, as if watching a hologram; the whole meeting

182 • *Cortina Jackson*

playing in a loop. He seemed to be going crazy as he entertained himself, watching something that was not there.

The death toll rose in the passing weeks from the flu. However, there did not seem to be a push to flee to the underground bunkers that the elites prepared. John sat day after day, quietly, waiting for orders, waiting for the tingle that he always felt when he knew it was time to kill. Suddenly, the hologram of his Chief discussing the elements of the meeting turned into a conversation directed at John. The Chief seemed to turn and speak to him directly.

"Biggs, all hands on deck, we have a crisis on our hands. We are having to do some crowd control. People are panicking and getting out of hand. Get your uniform on, and get downtown, bring every weapon that you got, it's going to get ugly out there."

"But I can't go," John announced, "I'm sick. I got the flu."

Suddenly John could see that the scientist, and the doctor reappeared beside the Chief in the corner. He sat shivering, unable to determine what was real, and what was delirium.

"We all are," the scientist said. "Something has gone wrong. It is time for us to go."

"Time to go where?" John asked. "What is the secret word that we are supposed to hear?"

"There is no time to explain," the doctor said. "People are sick that are not supposed to get sick. They are demanding answers; it is out of control. Now get up and let's go!"

John dragged his feet across the floor to his room to put on a police uniform that was only worn by detectives in an emergency. He felt weak, his pulse slowing to almost nothing, causing him to feel dead inside, and sicker than he had ever felt in his life. He had the chills, and his body ached, but he managed to put the wrinkled uniform on his unwashed body that stunk from days of dried vomit, urine, and blood.

The drive downtown was strange. The highways and freeways that were always packed, lending bumper to bumper traffic were now wide open. No cars were on the highway. It looked like an apocalypse, with cars abandoned on the roads, stores that appeared empty but looted, and no people in sight.

That is, until he approached the heart of downtown. It looked as though the whole city of Houston converged in one area. It took John forever, just to find an opening close enough to park, so that he could join the awaiting mayor, police officers, detectives, and commissioners and chiefs from surrounding precincts. John spotted Detective Chris from his bureau, and approached him, dodging trash and shoves directed at him from the angry mob. One of the commissioners approached the microphone that was set up for a press conference, as every news crew zeroed in, and held onto every word spoken.

The microphone squealed as the commissioner nervously adjusted it.

"As you all know, we have had an outbreak of the flu virus that has shut our city down. We don't want anyone to panic. We have been assured by the CDC that these cases are contained, and we have found a trial vaccine that is already curing some of the recipients. However, we want to make sure that the bug out there is quarantined to stop this virus in its tracks. It is going to take the patience and cooperation of all of you. We want to get everyone tested and treated. I ask that each of you return to your homes, as you are only making the virus spread faster by being here. Go home, we will assemble teams that will go door-to-door, quarantine individuals that have the sickness, get them treated and returned to their families."

"Why does it only seem to be affecting the affluent neighborhoods?" one of the reporters asked, as the crowd backed him with their loud chants of "Yeah!"

"Look who is out here right now, in the heart of downtown," the commissioner said. "Everyone else is at home, locked down. You guys are only spreading it faster and picking it up from each other to take back to your families."

Another reporter shouted his question, "Why is this so-called flu being called the Zombie Virus? Is it really turning people into zombie-infectious vectors?"

The detectives and constituents under Chief Brakeen's tutelage all turned at once and began heading to their vehicles. The trigger words had been used. At first, they walked with a purpose, getting to their vehicles as quickly and quietly as possible, and then they ran, as more of the crowd began moving toward their vehicles or any modes that they could use to get away from the area as soon as possible. The Chief spotted John and motioned for him to get in his car.

"I need for you to drive John, I know the coordinates to the location that we are to go. Just drive and I will direct you there."

John slid into the Chrysler with the Chief, Detective Chris, and two other detectives from the team. Behind their vehicle was a convoy of the other team members and members from the C6 Order in their black SUVs, which included the doctors, scientists, and others involved. John could hardly see as he seemed to be getting sicker. Everyone in the car was sick and coughing so hard that one of them was sure to expel a lung.

"What is happening to us?" John asked the Chief. "Why are we getting sick, we took the serum? Aren't we the elite, goddammit?"

The Chief's eyes were red, the whites of his eyes were no longer visible, and blood seemed to be weeping from them.

"Our operation did not go as planned. When the new flu virus was created, we used vectors that would wake up the dormant gene in people and create a new virus that would essentially turn everyone into these zombie-like creatures that we are seeing.

What was not taken into consideration was pre-existing immunity in the populations that we were trying to destroy. Pre-existing immunity happens when people are exposed to viruses, and their body sets up an immunity the next time they are exposed. It weakens the effectiveness of the new virus. The pre-existing immunity that people had, reduced the efficiency of virus re-administration, rendering the administration useless."

"English!" John yelled.

"For years pollutants have been dumped into water supplies; and genetically altered food was introduced all over the world, as the scientist explained. People suffered high blood pressure, diabetes, cancers, depression, autism, and other ailments. Medication was made to combat these ailments, but the medications themselves had side effects, and required additional medication to deal with the new occurring problems.

Over the years people became resilient, and their bodies built up an immunity. Now that a new strain of flu has been introduced, it has made them sick, but not enough to destroy them.

We took the blood, the organs, and the tissues of these resilient people, combined with altered genetic material that was introduced into our bodies, thinking it would make us even stronger. Obviously, it did not work for us, because we were not as resilient. We were not exposed to the ill-effects that were intended to weaken and wipe out people years ago.

So we never built up an immunity. Our bodies have become overloaded with foreign material that was not a part of our genetic makeup, and it is fighting against us, leaving us unable to fight off the new virus that is attacking our bodies. We are becoming weaker. They will become stronger."

"So what about all that bullshit talk from Dr. Fritz? I thought they harnessed the best qualities for our use. These are supposed to be top-notch scientist, and doctors. How could this happen?" John asked.

"I don't know the answers right now, but I am sure there are safeguards in place to protect us," the Chief tried to sound reassuring.

"Well here's what I think," John said angrily. "I think that the vector that they introduced to select subjects, that turned them into mind-controlled super assassins, were us. We are really the mind-controlled puppets. We are the so-called cockroaches, aren't we?"

The Chief remained quiet, as he looked out of his window at the chaos that whizzed by.

"Is there a cure, like the commissioner told everyone," John asked gripping the steering wheel tightly.

"I don' know John, ok. I don't have answers for you right now. I am told that there are secret bunkers away from society in case of mass hysteria, or some type of apocalypse. We will know when we get there. This new virus is extremely contagious, but I am sure there are vaccines that will cure us quickly. Just drive the damn car, please!"

"Oh you knew a lot, before all of this happened, didn't you? Our mighty monarch patriarch! Un-freaking-believable! We are turning into goddamn zombies. I hope that I am still dreaming right now."

John shook his head, his jaw tightly clenched. He glanced at the Chief for confirmation of his suspicions.

The Chief didn't speak any further, he just kept looking at his phone for the coordinates as they continued to drive for hours, going to a place that seemed non-existent. There were many vehicles traveling along the highway. They were from all over the place, as there were license plates from every state. Everyone was trying to escape it seemed, but going to the same place seemed to be ludicrous in everyone's present condition.

The three detectives in the back continued to cough, and after hours of weakness they neglected to cover their mouths or blow their noses. Their skin was very pale, and the two detectives with access to outside seats, both leaned over onto their windows, leaving bloody sputum on the glass. Detective Chris sat in the middle, he stared into the mirror from the back seat, his breathing was erratic.

"I figure now is just a good a time as any, to tell you some things." Chris spoke up.

John matched his gaze in the mirror.

"What?" John asked, anticipating the worse.

"Don't do this Chris, let's just get to where we are going, and preserve our energy" interrupted the Chief.

"I know who your real father is," Chris said, looking over at the back of the Chief's head. "I knew your little whore mother too."

John turned his head completely around to stare at Chris, while the car slid back and forth over the road, and the tires skidded and smoked from the friction.

"Kyle didn't love you, he was assigned to you, he handled you; but he started to get away from what he was told to do, and we had to get rid of him." Chris turned his head and coughed violently. "You're not a good cop or a good detective, you are a trained detective, doing whatever you are told to do."

The Chief jumped in, "Chris, that's enough!" as the car suddenly skidded to a stop. "We're here, let's deal with this later."

They found themselves in the dessert, somewhere near northeastern Arizona they presumed, indicated by some of the signs that they passed. There were cars everywhere. It seemed as though millions of people were already out of their cars, and standing in the middle of a vast barren area.

John jumped out of the car and met Chris at the door as he exited the vehicle. The hard impact against Chris' nose made a crunch underneath John's knuckle. Chris's nose began to bleed profusely as he grabbed it, trying to wipe tears and blood out of his eyes.

"Stop it, stop it now!" the Chief yelled. "We have to get going, and we have to conserve our energy or we will not make it, as we are already sick and weak."

"I would have no qualms about killing you right now," John said, looking at Chris, who was leaning against the car with both hands covering his nose.

People from everywhere were here, knowing their assignments led them to this place to take refuge from an uncertain existence in the cities and towns plagued with the flu. These were the elite; the ones who worked hard, and contributed to society, making it a better place again, so they deserved to be here. They were going to be part of the solution.

They moved as a unit, walking to their new destination. They were all very sick and irritated as they moved through the cacti and thickets that stuck into their legs as they brushed past them. They heard the constant warnings from rattlesnakes that didn't appreciate their area being invaded. Some of the men, women, and children were falling over, as they could push no further. The warm day was turning into a very cold dusk.

John, the chief, Detective Chris, and dozens of others moved along steadily for what seemed like hours. They could see a faint light that lit the sky beyond some hills that they were at the brink of climbing. John looked around to see that all those present seemed to be changing drastically. Everyone appeared to drag their feet, drool running from their mouths, and their gait was unsteady and hunched over.

They were all sick, hungry, and now angry that the location was such a feat that they did not anticipate. People began to argue with each other, which led to some all-out brawls that took turns for the worse. Skin was being ripped underneath fingernails, bones were being cracked underneath the heavy thud of a steel toed boot or spiked high heel. As they continued up the hill, thousands of people already looked like the living dead, with flesh hanging, dragging broken limbs, and moaning with pain, and weakness.

After what seemed like an eternity, they finally reached the other side, and saw a clearing with the brightest lights they had ever seen. It was so blinding that they had to shade their eyes, even though the darkness had fallen. They could hear loud shrieks over a sound system, like the deathcore fry scream at a death metal concert.

On a huge stage stood a steering committee of the top-secret society in the United States. They seemed to be chanting, as they said phrases repeatedly. Their voices did not sound human, as they welcomed everyone there.

"We the elite, who stand, and vowed our bodies to be sacrificed, and be scattered in six pieces if we ever revealed ourselves, are here," they chanted over and over again, in a disturbing, pig-like squeal.

It was unbearable to hear, and invoked fear among all the constituents of the conglomerate. Suddenly, a man in a huge, dark-colored robe seem to come from the shadows and appeared on the stage. The guttural growl of his voice was chilling as he spoke.

"Brothers and sisters, we are here to take our place to begin a better world, better than any of us has ever known. We have word from the Elite Council, they have pre-recorded a message that I will now play. This message will reveal our new destination. Do not worry my family, you will all receive the treatment that you need, and we will rule and reign forever, we the Elite."

Although they were weak, and near death, everyone cheered, at the exciting potential of a new life that had been promised to them.

"We have prayed to our god, and he has answered. Others have prayed to a God in heaven, and where are they now? Hahaha, they are in their inner cities dying; killing each other, looting, destroying everything, while we are here. Let them continue to kill each other, as we take our place in our great underworld," the cloaked man screamed into the microphone.

"And now, we shall hear from the Elite Council," he said as he played the live feed from the Elite Council that were already in the underground city built deep underneath the Earth.

It was a great nation that spanned many states, and was built with an intricate ventilation system, food, and resources to sustain every elite member and their families for many years. Everyone got quiet, as they stared at the stage where four cloaked men stood with their heads hidden deep within their hoods. They now tucked their hands in their robes, and lowered their heads, as they too listened for orders.

"You have all served faithfully going about your daily lives, doing your part to help build or add to this great nation. Drillers, architects, geological researchers, and archeologists, you have helped to build this great underground dwelling that we reside in now, thank you, your wisdom has been noble.

Every one of you have played a part in this great plan for worldwide domination, and with this power, we are able to enjoy the best of the best, forevermore. Your Orders, Societies, Sects, and Clubs, have helped us to grow in power, as we snuffed out the weak, the poor, the sick, the criminal. Your efforts have all been commendable. You have helped to purge a society that was only keeping us divided, and now we are all powerful, we reign, we are immortal, hahaha…!" The great voice spoke with purpose and drive.

"We are comfortably set in our kingdom now; we the 1 percent. Hahahaha…"

"You fools, the kingdom was not intended for you, the 10 percent. It was only for the 1 percent, the true Elite."

The crowd began to get restless and confused about the tone the voice now took, as loud coughs and moans were heard throughout the crowd. They continued to listen; however, to see where the Elite Council was going with the speech.

"You have all done a wonderful job, helping us to rid the world of the 89 percent of the population, and now you are gathered here to die. You, the so-called elite 10 percent, will destroy yourselves, and the others who remain. We are not in the United States; you are all so ignorant. We left the United States years ago to reside in our remote location.

We have left you to do the dirty work; to declare wars on other nations, to spread hate among all lands, to bankrupt this nation, and to kill each other. You are not beneficial to us anymore; your puppet strings have been cut. Hahaha… may you all burn in Hell." The voice was gone.

The cloaked men, threw off their hoods to expose their faces to the angry mob who had contracted the zombie-flu, and had no serotonin, or patience at this point, to keep them from going mad. John looked around wildly at the people around him.

"You used me, and for what?" he said addressing the Chief.

He looked at Detective Chris, "You knew, you all knew, and you said nothing, you let this son-of-a-bitch turn us into killers."

The crowd began to turn into a dangerous mob, as several people rushed the stage to tear the Elite apart for directing them to their place of death. Their crazed stares were spine-tingling, as their eyes took on a demon-like appearance. The creatures of fiction were not as far-fetched as the world had believed, as each person began to change into the hideous zombies far more terrifying than Hollywood had portrayed.

Creatures that should have never been seen by the eyes of another man, for their appearance was demonic, was now manifested. Now enveloped in the darkness of the night, people could only see glimpses of demons that now overtook each person. Their teeth were not human, they were long, and extended out of their mouths like fangs, and their eyes had turned into red snakelike slits glowing against the night. These people had become beasts, demons, and zombies, turning their animalistic behaviors on each other.

However, the destruction here was not isolated; for the same destruction intended for 99 percent of the world, would now be carried out in the 1 percent who now rested comfortably deep underground of the Ural Mountains.

A great city had been constructed deep within the crust of the Earth featuring a ventilation system that functioned as lungs, inhaling the air from above to pipe through intricate ventilation chambers circulating throughout the city. They were so deep within the Earth's crust that they could feel the warmth the Earth's core provided.

A toast was presented at the round table. For they had successfully destroyed mankind. Just as glasses were raised, a great rumble was felt that caused a shattering earthquake to erupt. The great vast city, constructed of the finest materials made to withstand the most extreme conditions, gave way to the Earth's movement. Suddenly the bottom of the underground city cracked, exposing molten lava that bubbled and spewed, permeating the great city.

There arose a voice so shrill and hideous that everyone fell onto their knees with a sickening weakness that rendered them useless.

"Hahaha! Welcome to Hell," the voice pierced through the souls of all inhabitants of the underground city.

The inhabitants fell to the bottom of Hell at the feet of Maniac. The head of the Elite Council stood before Maniac with pride.

"Master, I have done what you asked of me. I brought the world to its knees, soon they will all join us in Hell. I ask to continue to roam the Earth, as there is still work to be done."

Maniac, tasted the air with his forked tongue, as he narrowed his slitted eyes until they were a piercing stare that shredded the very soul of the head of the Elite Council; a stare that made him swoon with trembling fear.

Maniac grabbed him viciously by the throat; his hand burned through the skin until his hand was melted inches into the man's neck.

"You fool! You failed! You may have destroyed those puppets and minions who greedily hung onto your every word and whim like nescient imbeciles; but you left a society of people who will prevail. There were praying people, everywhere. They saw right through your evil intentions and took immediate action. The same media that was intended to robotize people was used to spread the word of your dealings. The harm you thought you were doing in introducing harmful vectors into the bodies of people made them more resilient.

The lack of faith in humanity you thought was apparent in people, due to the sick and twisted deeds of vile men, made them run to Him more. They rebuked us, they made us flee, and they defeated us. Now the world is rid of the diabolicalness meant to destroy them. They will emerge from their homes unscathed, stronger than ever, and will come together to re-build a nation that trusts God, because you could not do your job correctly!"

Maniac squeezed tighter, his hand melting deeper into the man's throat, burning through his windpipe and soldering his throat closed. He held the man up staring at him, contemplating what to do with him next.

Another demon stepped forward, to speak for the head Elite Councilman.

"Master, we can go back and influence the rest of them. Yes, they will emerge from their homes and unite. They will realize that they need each other, and together they stand but divided they fall, but not everyone left believes.

There will still be hatred, desire for control, murder and mayhem. We will go back stronger and take more demons with us. You will rule the Earth again Master, we will see to it!" the demon spoke, crawling around on claws as his body moved back and forth like a serpent.

Maniac released the councilman, who fell to the ground, and took on its original form, a hideous demon with three co-bra heads, 12 arms that extended out as tentacles that free-floated like an apparition; each tentacle had dozens of eyeballs on it. The tentacles pierced anything near them with electricity that surged through its victim, so that he could pull the victim into its mouth, located in its abdomen, fixed with rows of razor sharp teeth

The demon laid at Maniac's feet, looking up into Maniac's disapproving stare that locked onto to his like a blazing inferno.

"Go back, and take this miserable beast with you," Maniac said, as he delivered a kick into the abdomen of the demon that lay at his feet, shattering teeth that were sent deep into the belly of the beast, causing him to scream out in horrific pain.

"Our time is upon us, I do not want hope, peace, and trust to ruin our plan. Snuff it out, immediately!" Maniac spoke.

The great underground city was no more, engulfed in molten liquid that bubbled up and consumed the screaming souls already tortured in Hell. Souls were dipping underneath the lava and springing up, choking on the thick fiery liquid, and convulsing from the flames that tortured their bodies. Their bodies boiled up and down like a bubbling pot of beans. Burned out eyes were wide open, and mouths wider, as they screamed in torment and torture.

***

John felt the rush of raw emotion and anger that fueled his own boiling inferno, churning in his belly, and entering into his throat as he yelled, alarming everyone around him. He grabbed Detective Chris by the throat, and with both hands squeezed until he heard a crack, and felt bones displaced underneath his hands. Chris fell to the ground. He then looked into the eyes of the chief.

"And you," he said. "You bastard, you manipulated all of us, you turned me into a killer. Your hatred for people was shared by so many, even me. You promised us a better way of life, an escape from all the animals of society, but we were the animals all along. Look at us, we're the monsters."

The chief displayed a cocky confidence as he smiled at John with an arrogant grin.

"Don't you see John, you and I are the same. We think the same, we act the same, and we kill the same. I am you, and you are me!"

John could contain his anger no longer, he quickly grabbed the chief by his shoulders and pushed him to the ground, as he bit at the side of his neck, ripping and tearing the flesh from it, swallowing huge chunks of flesh.

Suddenly, out of nowhere, John felt his body lift from the ground, and he was hurled back down with a thud. Five crazed men with blood pouring from their mouths began to take bites out of his body, eating him alive. They ripped and tore whatever flesh that they could get. John made a gurgled, breathless outcry, as blood was squeezed into his throat.

"We're the monsters, we're the monsters, we're the monsters…"

Chapter 19

Suddenly, with a huge gasp of air that he seemed to fight to obtain, John raised his body to free his lungs from their near collapse. He couldn't raise up fully, as he noticed that he was handcuffed to a hospital bed. He looked around, his eyes were as big as a starless galaxy. He expected to find himself eaten and torn apart, but instead he found himself in an all-white sterile room.

"They're for your protection," an older looking nurse said in a monotone voice, without even looking at John. "You split your head open again; and yes, you are a monster!" She shook her head, and walked out of the room in disgust, burned out with her job.

John turned his head slightly from side to side and winced in pain as he felt a gash in the back of his head. He didn't attempt to move any further as he lay there vulnerable and confused. Feeling lethargic, and listless, he closed his eyes again.

He spent weeks in the medical department; continuing to drift in and out of consciousness, wondering if he was dreaming, or already dead. Sitting in a chair across from a beautiful doctor made him realize that he was still alive. He sat there wondering how exactly he got there and when, as he stared into her concerned eyes. She looked down at her writing pad, as she slipped on a pair of reading glasses. She appeared to be studying her notes intensely before looking up and removing them.

"It's called Dissociative Identity Disorder," she said.

"What?" John said, blinking, wondering why medical terms were suddenly being hurled at him.

"Dissociative Identity Disorder, split personality," she repeated. "We have talked about this many times John. Am I speaking with John right now, or Chief Brakeen, or is it Dark Man?"

"What are you talking about?" John asked, as his headache began to creep upon him with a hard ache, which made his whole body tremble uncontrollably.

"John you have developed alter egos, as a way of dealing with your abuse, and I fear that you have taken on a few more."

"I am a detective with the Houston Police Department, Homicide Division," John said.

"No, I am Chief Brakeen, with the Houston Police Department. John is a murderer, and a coward, I have proof," the Chief spoke from John's lips. "He killed his father, and many others."

"No John, no you are not. You are John Doe, the serial killer, coined as the Silent Night Killer," the doctor interrupted. "You killed your adopted father, a police officer; and countless other people under the cover of your badge. You are one of the most notorious serial killers this world has ever seen. Your final appeal is at risk of being denied; we are trying to save you from the death penalty, as the courts are seeking. I am here to help you, so that at least you can avoid prison, and continue to spend your life at a facility getting the treatment that you need. You can't continue smashing your head onto the concrete floor, so that you can escape death; otherwise, you will end up dead at your own doing."

Correctional Officer Chris Parnell, knocked on the door with his riot baton, and entered the room.

"Time is up doctor, he has to get back to his cell."

"Just a few more moments officer, please." The doctor asked. She turned back and looked at John, "John please no more head banging, or they will put you in five-point restraints, and you will lie there all day."

"Come on, monster," Officer Chris said, laughing at the situation unprofessionally.

He took the handcuffs off the bar that chained John to the table; which separated him and the doctor, and attached them behind his back, as he walked him back to his cell.

"What am I doing here, I thought I killed you already, Detective Chris Kelley! How are you still alive? How did I end up in prison? How did I get caught?" John asked, seeing the image of the detective create a transition from one image to another.

"Wow, those cracks to your head really are making you stupid," the guard said, "and for the one hundredth time, my name is Officer Chris Parnell, genius. How many times do we have to go through this? You were sloppy and were identified by a couple of victims that got away.

Joyce Anderson, a former police officer, became a huge advocate for justice, and helped solve the numerous murders that you committed. She was instrumental in bringing the whole corrupt police department down, including the Chief, who you pretend to be; and her efforts contributed to catching the most notorious serial killer in Texas, 'The Silent Night Killer.' She is now the commissioner of Houston.

I wish Texas still had the electric chair, and they could fry your ass; but I am content with them pumping your body with drugs, that will stop your cold inhumane heart."

He whispered, as he removed the handcuffs, and gave John a hard push with his baton through the narrow tray slot.

"Oh, and please stop cracking your head on the ground, I'm tired of mopping up your venomous blood. Let's make this a silent night, shall we?" He laughed hysterically, as he walked away.

John fell over onto the cold floor, but quickly righted himself, and stood up rubbing his wrists, which now bore the deep red impressions of tight handcuffs. He walked over and laid on his side on the concrete slab, only separated by the thin blue mat issued to him. He closed his eyes, wishing that he was dead.

Perhaps another crack to his head would ensure his death this time. His thoughts would not be quiet, as he heard voices that clouded his mind, and made his head spin. He began to hallucinate, as blood poured from his ears, and nose. He didn't bother to clean it up or wipe it away, it streamed down his face and dripped onto the blue mat.

He constantly thought that he sat before his Chief, the detectives, his victims, his mother, his doctor; but he never moved from his state of repose on his concrete slab.

"John," he could hear the doctor say, "I think that we can convince the courts to let us try cognitive behavioral therapy with you. We will be able to look at your unhealthy patterns and thought processes, and with work, we can develop diverse ways of thinking. I would also like to try a new drug on you that we have been testing, to help go along with the therapy."

John lay there, "No, no drugs," he mumbled.

He could now hear his mom's voice.

"Get up you little loser, I should just kill you myself, you worthless little bastard. Kill yourself, John."

"I am a loser, and an animal, and a monster." John said.

"No, you're not, John." John could hear the voice of Officer Joyce Anderson.

"I'm praying for you, John. You're hurt, your head is bleeding, and you're coughing up blood. Our Father which are in Heaven hallowed be thy name, thy Kingdom come, thy will be done on Earth as it is In Heaven," she continued to pray over her wounded friend.

"Stop praying for me, what the hell is wrong with you?" he shouted.

"John, will you accept Jesus Christ as your personal savior? He will help you now. No matter what you have done, God will forgive you," he heard her say.

"Hell no, you go way, and leave me alone. I'm guilty, I want to die," he yelled at her, but there was no one there.

Other voices overwhelmed his thoughts, until he could not formulate a complete thought on his own.

"He has exhausted all of his appeals. His fate is in God's hands now," he heard another voice faintly come through.

Voices continued to come and go, images long suppressed came into view clearly. Thoughts that he wanted to forget were now vivid memories that haunted him. He was never the fine upstanding police officer that he thought he was. He just imagined that having power, control, and respect would make him better than the evil and deadly serial killer that he had become.

Realization of who he truly was made him angrier, and he knew that he wanted to kill again, and if he had the opportunity to do it, he would follow through; he felt it burning in his cold-hearted chest like a hot ember in snow.

"John Doe, John, open your eyes, are you with us? He's waking up," a reassuring voice slowly became clearer, and more distinct.

John awakened to find himself surrounded by powder blue walls, which looked like an open sky; and blurry figures that seemed to scramble around him in warp speed.

"Am I in Heaven?" John inquired.

"No, you are not," a voice spoke. "Let us proceed."

A curtain slid open to John's right, revealing rows of people that he could hardly make out, and he found himself strapped to a table. A microphone was positioned overhead, which jutted out from the cinderblock wall that held it in place, to capture and project final words.

"This is John Doe Bigsby. Mr. Bigsby you have the opportunity to make a final statement if you wish at this time." A voice was projected into the tiny room, where John was now alone.

John smiled, as he saw a faint reflection of himself in the thick glass that separated him from his on-lookers. Appearing back was the reflection of pure evil, with an unapologetic heart that was beating against his chest with deep thuds. John turned his head at once to stare back into the ceiling that he hoped to move beyond in a matter of minutes.

"It's finally over Warden, I'm finally free," John spoke.

"I have been asked where all of those missing children are." John continued, as he looked back at the faint figures beyond the glass window with a smile.

"They are inside of people who reaped their benefits, they live on. I did them a favor, they hated this life, and were worthless. They are much more useful now," John chuckled. "I get the liberty of death, I sure feel sorry for all of y'all left here to live, under someone else's control. Is that living? Let's get this over with Warden." John smiled, and closed his eyes, indicating that he rendered his final statement.

John felt the sting of the hot Pentobarbital that suddenly coursed through his veins. He began to slip away into the darkness, as the drug began to warm his entire body. John was soon enveloped in a quiet, dark, peace. However, the peace would be short-lived, as his body temperature elevated to the point of burning, which made John open his eyes wide in shock and pain.

"Ha, ha, ha, ha!!! Welcome to Hell," Maniac said, with a toothy grin, as he slowly raised his arms, and looked around him to welcome John to his new fate.

Dark Man now appeared. He was a tall black shadowy demon, with bulging glowing eyes, and long black fingers that had marionette strings hanging from them. He seemed to emerge from John's very soul, and he now stared down at John's paralytic body.

"Good work, our little puppet," the demons both said in unison, as they taunted John.

Soon, imps and demons began to pick the flesh off of John's body, as he screamed in terror and torment. His eyes and mouth were opened wide, like a deep, dark sepulcher. His screams only blended in with the others, who also screamed from the pain of being boiled up and down in the thick ignited lava.

John cowered in fear, as Maniac now moved in close to his ear; his hideous tongue darting in and out, sliding around on

John's face. The demon laughed, but abruptly ceased as he slid his tongue back into his mouth, eyes narrowing, as he stood up and spoke loudly.

"Soon, other manipulated, mind-controlled people will join you from the Earth. They do not take us seriously. They do not believe we exist. They have given up on their beliefs. Our job will be much easier now. Hahaha…"

Maniac continued, "The world is screaming loudly for justice and peace, while no one is being heard, as they selfishly scream from their own homes. With our efforts to keep everyone divided, and our evil deeds hidden in plain sight, we will fulfill *our* agenda. The sounds of silence will continue to be the loudest."

John shrieked in sheer trepidation as he was dragged away by the imps, but not before he heard Maniac began to whistle the best rendition of "Silent Night" he had ever heard, good enough to earn him a Grammy.

An order is given in Hell for evil forces to emerge upon the Earth to do, "On Earth as it is in Hell." What happens next is pure evil.

Life is scarier than fiction; the fate of the world is scarier than this!

Available now at

www.cortinajackson.com

E-book available at Amazon.com

www.ingramcontent.com/pod-product-compliance
Lightning Source LLC
Chambersburg PA
CBHW031421250626
47155CB00004B/1578